The Canning Season

All the way down the cliff and into the water Ratchet wondered if Tilly and Penpen had actually seen That Thing. If they hadn't seen it, what would they say when they saw it today? In the back of her mind, like a tiny minuscule guarded thread of hope, was the thought that maybe her mother had been wrong and people wouldn't mind so much, that it wasn't quite as grotesque as Henriette thought. That Penpen and Tilly had seen it and simply not thought that much about it. If that was the case, she didn't mind taking off her things. On the other hand, suppose they were going to see it now for the first time. In that case, she'd rather not take anything off. She would just rather not swim.

ALSO BY POLLY HORVATH

Everything on a Waffle

The Canning Season

POLLY HORVATH

■SCHOLASTIC

Melissa Public Library
Melissa, Texas

Scholastic Children's Books,
Euston House, 24 Eversholt Street
London, NW1 1DB, UK
a division of Scholastic Ltd
London ~ New York ~ Toronto ~ Sydney ~ Auckland
Mexico City ~ New Delhi ~ Hong Kong

First published in the US by Farrar Straus Giroux, 2003
Published in the UK by Scholastic Ltd, 2006

Copyright © Polly Horvath, 2003

10 digit ISBN 0 439 95955 1
13 digit ISBN 978 0439 95955 1

All rights reserved

Printed by Nørhaven Paperback A/S, Denmark

10 9 8 7 6 5 4 3 2 1

The right of Polly Horvath to be identified as the author of this work
has been asserted by her in accordance with the
Copyright, Designs and Patents Act, 1988.

This book is sold subject to the condition that it shall not, by way of trade or
otherwise, be lent, resold, hired out, or otherwise circulated without the
publisher's prior consent in any form of binding or cover other than that in
which it is published and without a similar condition, including this condition,
being imposed upon the subsequent purchaser.

Papers used by Scholastic Children's Books are made from wood grown in
sustainable forests.

Melissa Public Library
Melissa, Texas

To Arnie, Emmy, Becca, Keena and Zayda

CONTENTS

Prologue   1
Mrs Menuto Loses Her Head   7
Myrtle Trout   20
The Graves   34
Tilly's Brief But Oddly
    Satisfying Marriage   44
The Blueberry Business   56
Harper   69
Dr Richardson's Long Arm   95
The Gardening Hat   116
Harper Two   140
That Thing   151
The Canning Season   178
Epilogue   187

PROLOGUE

Ratchet Clark lived with her mother, Henriette, in a small, gloomy sub-basement apartment in Pensacola, Florida. They had no windows, but if they had she imagined they would be able to see worms, grubs, and strange scary insects. There would be larvae eating the corpses that people had snuck into the apartment yard to bury under cover of night. Only her and her mother's thin bedroom walls separated them from this place of nightmares.

Ratchet never slept well, but Henriette did. She snored loudly as soon as she hit the pillow. Ratchet worried about her, worn out as she always was from waiting tables at the Hunt Club and cleaning other people's apartments. She sometimes dreamt of these creatures making their way through the wall in the middle of the night, worms drilling small holes, slipping through, getting into her mother's skull via her ears. She woke often, listening for the sound of small, industrious insects. Sometimes these dreams were so real that she'd awake the next morning and stare worriedly at Henriette's ears, looking for evidence, searching for tiny holes. Once when Henriette caught her at this she said, "Don't stare at me that way. How can I take you to the Pensacola Hunt Club? They'll think you're a halfwit!"

The Pensacola Hunt Club with its horses, tennis, swimming, and sumptuous clubhouse had been Henriette's beacon of light for the last thirteen years. She coveted a membership. She didn't own a horse and didn't ride, but she would bring home riding pants, crops and helmets, the things that made her appear as if she did.

"The Pensacola Hunt Club!" she'd say, striding around the house with her riding crop tucked underneath her arm. She wore big black riding boots that reached almost to her knees. Her skin bulged over the top like kneesocks turned over. It wasn't very elegant, but fortunately she didn't look down very often. She thought she looked simply topping.

"How do I look today, Ratchet?" she would ask, and if Ratchet didn't say "Simply topping" an icy silence would prevail.

That night, as the gloom of night descended, which it did even earlier in their sub-basement than in the rest of Florida, they sat about the kitchen table having their Ovaltine and Cheerios. It was silent in the apartment. Henriette had no friends and was hardly ever home, and Ratchet was not allowed to make friends.

"Don't hold your spoon like that, Ratchet! The Hunt Club! The Hunt Club!" said Henriette suddenly. Then Henriette repeated what she always did. "Thank God for the Hunt Club!"

"Yes, the Hunt Club!" Ratchet agreed as usual.

"Thank God for that!"

"Yes!"

"Where would we be without it?"

"Nowhere, that's where."

"Well, thank God for it."

"Yep, that's for sure," Ratchet said hopefully, and then Henriette's eyes went stony again and the house returned to silence.

Ratchet found the whole idea of the Hunt Club comforting, its lushness having been described to her since she was a baby. She wanted to go there with Henriette, but Henriette said that it wasn't a good idea because of That Thing on Ratchet's shoulder blade and how it would reflect on her, Henriette. "And I wish I had given you a different name," she said, sighing. "That was your father's fault."

"Did he choose my name?" asked Ratchet.

Henriette shrugged and looked impatient. "I was young. It's just one of those things you do when you're young."

Ratchet had never seen her father. He had taken a powder after her birth.

"I'd just given birth, which is a frightful experience. Nothing prepares you for it. They won't even let you *eat* until it's all over. No matter how *hungry* you get, they won't let you do anything but breathe. I didn't want to breathe. I wanted a *hamburger*! And then, when it's all over and they finally do bring you something to eat, it's really yucky."

"What did they bring *you*?"

"I don't remember, Ratchet. Chicken in cream sauce probably. That's the only thing they ever serve for dinner in the hospital. They may call it by another name, they may say, for instance, it's ham bake or Salisbury steak, but it's really always chicken in cream sauce."

Ratchet salivated. They hadn't had anything like chicken in cream sauce in a long time. Ham bake and Salisbury steak sounded pretty good, too. They'd been living on Cheerios since Henriette bought her new riding habit.

"OK, so then after I say take that baby away and bring me some chicken in cream sauce they wheel me into this room with seven other new mothers. Naturally, I make a fuss. I mean, if I wanted to hang out with a bunch of other women I would have lived on a commune, right? I would have had my labour in some touchy-feely ashram. So I kept pressing my call button over and over until they got me out of there. The nurses think I'm a little wacko, and believe me, at that point, after a whole day in the hospital with all those crummy smells, I practically am, and they move me into the only private room left, which happens to be empty because the pipes are being fixed in there. The workmen continue on the pipes because they say they have a work order, and while the nurse goes out to get someone bigger and stronger I get rid of them by throwing bits of placenta about."

"Bits of what?" Ratchet asked.

"Of course, it was really cherry Jell-O from my second dinner tray, but they didn't know that. They left in a hurry. Can you imagine putting workmen in a new mother's room? Anyhow, I'm about to heave a sigh of relief when I see one of them has left a tool on the window sill. Well, that's the last straw because it means somebody is going to come clomping in in the middle of the night to retrieve it. I didn't notice it at first because your father and I were deep in a fight over what to name you. It's very tense having a baby, you know, Ratchet. No one tells you what you're supposed to do with it once it's out of your stomach. It's just there! That's why new mothers are always forgetting and leaving their babies in the washrooms of public places. Because who can keep track *all the time*? Naming you should have been the easy part of the whole deal, but, of course, nothing was ever easy with your father. I liked the name Eugenie, and your father kept saying, 'STINKO. Let's name her STINKO.' Just to be funny. Can you imagine annoying me after the kind of day I'd had? Then he says, 'Or how about FART? FART Clark!'

"I'd say Yvonne, and he'd say Belch. He just wasn't listening, he was too busy being hilarious. That's when I saw the tool on the window sill. 'Who left that ratchet on the window sill?' I asked, but of course he can't just answer the question. He has to argue. 'No, it's not a ratchet, it's a lug wrench.' Well, I knew a ratchet when I saw one. So we're arguing away and he starts shouting. He could be so moody, Ratchet. You just never knew when he was going to erupt. It was quite frightening, really. And he threatens to wheel my bed to the window, crank it up, and tip me out if I don't admit it's a lug wrench. So I just pick up a magazine and pretend to read an article about polo ponies and ignore him. I always found that it was better to ignore him when he had moods.

" 'Ratchet,' I say airily as he cranks up the top part of the bed so that I begin to slip gently down those slippery hospital sheets toward the open window. And that's another thing, hospital sheets are made of some kind of synthetic fibre between polyester and nylon, so that patients are constantly slipping off their beds. Thud, thud, thud, you hear all night long in hospitals. Nine out of ten hospital patients break a bone while rolling over for a glass of water in the middle of the night. The other ten per cent die of heartbreak when they find out they don't have any water and what the chances are of getting some.

"Anyhow, 'Lug wrench,' says your father.

" 'Ratchet,' I say.

" 'Lug wrench,' he says.

"Just as my legs slide out the open fifth-floor window, my nightgown all bunched up and my bare thighs dangling in the breeze, a nurse comes racing in squealing, 'Oh, Mr Clark! Mrs Clark! If it's fresh air you want, you need only ask for a wheelchair!'

"Then she hauls me in and slams the window shut in case we forget and make that mistake again. Anyhow, I keep pretending to read, which drives your father crazy, and he's about to go on another rampage when he hears someone in the hall exclaim that Havana cigars are being passed out in the waiting room, and dashes off. While he's gone, a woman comes in for the birth certificate information and I grab the form and fill out Ratchet! Ratchet! in the space for the first and middle names, and that's how you became Ratchet Ratchet Clark. Oh, and by the way, you're going to Maine tonight."

MRS MENUTO LOSES HER HEAD

"I'm going where?" Ratchet gasped.

"Maine."

"Maine?" Ratchet cried. "Why am I going there?"

"You're spending the summer with great–second cousins, Tilly and Penpen Menuto. You can just call them aunts. I called them Aunt Tilly and Aunt Penpen, and they always referred to me as their niece. You can be a niece, too. Who says 'Great–second cousin once removed Tilly' or whatever it would be. It's too much of a mouthful. They're some distant relatives or other. I'd almost forgotten about them. I used to spend summers with them. You're old enough now to get some away-from-home experience, and that's the only free place I could think of."

"I'm going tonight? Why didn't you tell me before?"

"I thought it would make a nice surprise. Come on, hurry up, it's going to take two days to get there. I've got train and bus tickets for you. You'll like sleeping on the train. The clickety-clack and all that. Here's your itinerary. Hurry up, Ratchet, get your coat."

"But it's hot out," Ratchet said.

"Not in Maine. Don't they teach you anything in school?" Henriette was walking swiftly up the basement stairs to the parking lot. She drove purposefully with no idea where she was going. She had never been to the train station, but she figured, what the heck, she had a map. Henriette took the same routes through Pensacola and never deviated from her habitual courses. Within minutes they were lost. Ratchet clutched her seat nervously as Henriette, flustered that the streets weren't where she figured they should be, almost hit a pedestrian and ran a stop sign. It was at this point that Henriette remembered Ratchet's suitcase sitting at home.

"Too late," she said. "Too late. Damn it. Well, I'll try to remember to send you a few things." She swung into a convenience store to find someone who could tell them how to get to the train station, and they got there just minutes before the train pulled out.

"I didn't even know I *had* any relatives," Ratchet said as they hurried across the platform.

"They were already old when I spent summers with them. They must be casket-ready by now. Penpen was kind of fat and happy-happy all the time, and Tilly looked like a sphincter."

"Like a what?" Ratchet asked, but the conductor was hurrying her up the steps to the train. She and her mother didn't say goodbye. Her mother had long ago told her that in their family they were no good at hellos, no good at goodbyes, and not much good with the stuff in between. As Ratchet turned, she could hear her mother trying to shout something to her over the roar of the train starting up.

"*What?*" Ratchet called through the open train door.

"*Keep That Thing covered!*" Henriette cried and headed back to the parking lot.

Ratchet watched her mother's retreating form as long as she could, then went into the train car. People were already slumped and slumbering, their faces pressed against windows, or their heads hanging heavy on their chests. There weren't any seats next to women available, so she sat next to a man who was sound asleep and drooling slightly on his lapel. She felt a terrible wrench at being pulled away from her mother, like a boot being pulled out of thick mud with a great sucking sound. But she knew her mother would despise such feelings. They were fussy. She put her feet and knees together and her hands in her lap and kept this position pretty much all the way to Maine.

Tilly was tiny and very, very thin. Penpen was round and jolly, just as Henriette had said, and even though she had short white hair, she didn't look all that old. Not nearly as old as Tilly, but Ratchet knew that she must be because the first thing that Tilly said to her when she got in their waiting car was, "We are twins. We were born together, we grew up together, we have lived our whole lives together, and we have plans to die together. The thing is, as I tried to explain to your mother, who by the way—"

"We are living somewhere very remote," interrupted Penpen, flashing Ratchet a smile from the front seat.

"So if we die, you will be stuck, that's all I was trying to tell Henriette! But, as usual, she wasn't listening. Stuck," said Tilly glumly, putting on her driving gloves.

Tilly sat on two phone books and a cushion and yet she could barely see over the wheel. Ratchet sat in the back seat. It was black out. In fact, the night sky, the whole night air of the Maine woods, had an oily quality – a dark so deep you could almost see rainbows in it. Ratchet had no idea where she was. Her ticket said "Dairy", but Henriette had told her that her great-aunts had a house past Dink. All these "D" names blurred in her mind as they drove through tiny lit streets. Finally even the few lights of town were gone and she was too tired to track their journey further. Too tired to do anything but try to remain upright in the back seat and be polite.

"If something were to happen to one of us, as I *tried* to explain to your mother on the phone, you'd be sunk," Tilly went on.

"Unless you learn to drive the Daimler, of course."

"Your mother—"

"Oh, look, a bear!" said Penpen.

Ratchet pressed her face to the window to see the bear but saw nothing except more darkness, so she leaned back. The roads became narrower. Penpen asked if anyone wanted a brown bag, of which they kept a healthy supply up front "just in case". Ratchet reached a hand forward for one, but although Tilly's driving made her queasy she never needed to use it. Instead she fidgeted, twisting and untwisting it. Tilly drove twenty miles an hour and made many sudden jerky stops because she kept thinking she saw things in the dark. Penpen would crane her neck around, checking the car on all sides, before saying, "Drive on, Tilly." And Tilly would drive on until she saw the next mirage and jerked to another stop, and another, until they finally stopped for good beyond a gate with a sign reading GLEN ROSA.

The Menuto house was enormous, made from old brick and spouting a profusion of towers and turrets that reached up in line with the tops of the pines that encircled it to prick the vast starry sky. From the front yard, where Tilly stopped the car, Ratchet could hear the sound of the sea crashing on rocks somewhere below. She tripped sleepily toward the house. She had spent forty-eight hours travelling, most of them sleepless, and could barely keep track of her feet.

"Don't fall down the cliff," said Penpen, grabbing Ratchet's shirt between her shoulder blades and yanking her back. Ratchet was so tired that the sudden sight of white foam spraying below and the realization that she had almost joined it with a splash didn't startle her, but Penpen's hand on her shirt did. She immediately and instinctively jerked away, wondering if Penpen had felt That Thing through the thin fabric. But if she had, she registered nothing. Ratchet looked down after that and followed the white rock walkway up to the house. She was too tired to take any notice of her surroundings. All she could remember as she drifted off to sleep was climbing a large winding staircase and being shown to a room from where she could hear the sound of the sea even louder, banging its way toward shore and back. Why does it keep doing that? she thought; why can't it just shut up? and fell asleep in her underwear.

"The most immediate concern," said Tilly the next morning over waffles with raspberries — there seemed to be a great deal of raspberries around; there were baskets of them rotting all over the house — "is clothes. Most specifically, but not entirely, Penpen, summer clothes."

"Swimsuit," said Penpen.

"Shorts."

Underwear, thought Ratchet.

"She hasn't even a toothbrush!" said Tilly indignantly. "Her mother—"

"*Would* you like some more berries?" interrupted Penpen, passing a large bowl across the table to Ratchet.

"How did you sleep?" asked Tilly.

"Good," said Ratchet. It was the deepest sleep she could remember ever having. She had never slept above ground in an upstairs bedroom. There were no underground insects drilling small holes. She had awakened groggily in the middle of the night to see the wind off the ocean fluttering the yellow dotted-swiss curtains in front of her octagonal window. I have a porthole, she thought. She wanted to call Henriette and tell her. Ratchet tried to stay awake to watch the fluttering curtains in the light of a moon that emerged in the middle of the night, but she was too tired. Sometime during her sleep she had surrendered to the sound of the surf, the soothing waves, their deep rhythm creeping into her unconscious all night like the heartbeat of a large animal.

"Go out and get some air," said Penpen. "Tilly and I must tidy up and get our hats and then we will go make the necessary purchases in town."

Ratchet went outside to explore. The morning was bright, sunshine sparkling on the water, filtering through the pine trees. She didn't bother to put on her shoes but scrambled down the rocky edge of the cliff to dangle her feet in the sea. A seal swam by and a fishing boat chugged along in the distance. Sea gulls made a great deal of early-morning mindless noise. But it was all strange sounds, strange sights. These were not Florida gulls, they were strange northern gulls. Even with the porthole she did not want to be here and wondered if she would be able to keep her breakfast down.

"Come along," shouted Tilly from the cliff top. Ratchet ran up the cliff for her shoes.

"We're going into Dink, dear," said Penpen.

They climbed into the Daimler. Penpen, with a grimly sympathetic look, gave Ratchet a brown bag. Tilly still drove with a series of slow violent jerks, as if the car itself were heaving its way down the road, but Ratchet was distracted by seeing the countryside she hadn't been able to see the night before. First the dirt road ran inland through thick bushes that scratched against both sides of the Daimler. Then it widened and swampland appeared, and woods so deep it looked as if night had fallen permanently beneath them. Blueberry bushes grew everywhere in the swamps, and in the distance she saw a large animal drinking.

"Oh, look at the moose, Tilly!" said Penpen, which caused Tilly to drive off the road into a bush and it took fifteen minutes to manoeuvre the car back on to the road.

"Please do not point out any more wildlife, Penpen," said Tilly. "If we get stuck here, we'll be stuck for ever. None of us could walk all the way to town."

"I'm almost certain Ratchet could. You have good strong legs, don't you, Ratchet?" asked Penpen.

"I don't know," Ratchet said, looking down uncertainly at them. When Henriette saw them she always said, "There's your father's bony knees staring at me like a reproach."

"Even if she could walk it, it would only be to be eaten by a bear along the way," said Tilly.

"True, too true," said Penpen.

"There was that incident years ago."

"But that was *many* years ago," said Penpen.

"Yes," said Tilly and sighed as if the subject were closed. "You see, Ratchet, that's what I meant when I said that if we were to die and you were alone at Glen Rosa. . ."

"And could not drive. . ."

"And could not walk. . ."

"You'd be pretty much sunk."

"What about the telephone?" Ratchet asked.

"You can't call out, you can only get calls in," said Tilly. "Father fixed it that way the year after we first got the phone. It was because our mother developed a habit."

"She certainly did," said Penpen.

"She phoned everyone."

"The San Diego Zoo, people in China, proprietors of shops in Little Rock, Arkansas. She had this great curiosity about the world. It was a wonderful thing, really."

"And if Father had only let her travel I'm sure she would never have developed the habit. But he kept her here on our property, far from anything, and didn't even let her do the shopping."

"He thought it was undignified. A Menuto shopping! That's what servants were for."

"So she never got to go anywhere or meet anyone. It was a real tragedy."

"She's what people today would have called a people person," said Penpen.

"So at least she was spared that," said Tilly, "dying when she did. At such an early age."

"We were just girls, Tilly and I. Exactly your age, actually."

"How did she die?" Ratchet asked.

"She offed herself," said Penpen.

"What?" Ratchet said.

"She killed herself in a particularly brutish and horrible way. I don't know why. I suppose it was all she could come up with at the time. Or maybe she was experimenting. She was very imaginative."

"How did she do it?" Ratchet asked.

"She cut off her own head."

"Oh no!" said Ratchet.

"I suppose you think that's rather thrilling," said Penpen. "People think children are going to be upset by things that I'm sure they think are quite thrilling. Tilly and I were proud of her. It must have taken extreme nerve, wouldn't you say, Tilly?"

"It wasn't your ordinary way to go. Mother never did anything the ordinary way."

"Weren't you so sad?" asked Ratchet.

"Oh, we were," said Penpen, "for many many years. She was a wonderful woman, but she simply wasn't made to be closeted up like that. Anyhow, Father never bothered changing the phone line afterward. I guess he thought it would come in handy when we had swains. Not that things ever became very swainish around our house. Too far out. And so Tilly and I just kind of stayed on, and then when we were in our teens Father died. We dismissed the servants after that and buried Father in the backyard, and Tilly and I taught ourselves to drive."

"We never bothered with silly things like licences," said Tilly. "At the time you didn't need them."

"No, but it doesn't matter, of course," said Penpen.

"All these things that people 'out there' think you need that are complete hogwash. Anyhow, I reminded your mother when she phoned that we were in a very remote area and could really not take on the responsibility of a child. Not because we couldn't care for one but because we plan to die together, and if we suddenly do, then you'd be trapped out here. It isn't a pretty thought. But Penpen had to go and become a Zen Buddhist."

"Now, now," interrupted Penpen, "I wouldn't go that far. I haven't become anything but interested."

"*She* said," Tilly went on, "that we must take in whatever shows up. You cannot turn anyone away. Take in the whole world, these Buddhists do, if it shows up at their door."

"It's a lovely philosophy, and you see, there you were showing up, just as I was espousing it. Can there be any real accidents? Mustn't we trust in some kind of design to it all?"

"Good thing we don't live closer to town," grumbled Tilly. "We'd be eaten out of house and home. Vacuum cleaner salesmen would be moving in with us. What were those men that used to go door to door selling spices, Penpen? We haven't seen them in years and years. Raleigh men! We'd have Raleigh men in all the spare bedrooms. Just because they showed up at the door. It isn't a practical philosophy."

"I don't believe there are Raleigh men any more," said Penpen.

"Where did all the Raleigh men go?" asked Tilly.

"And even if there were Raleigh men and even if they showed up, I don't suppose they'd all want to stay."

"Makes no difference, I'm sure you'd be clunking them on the head and dragging them in anyway, Penpen."

"I'm really not like that," Penpen said to Ratchet.

And then they drove quietly, peacefully on.

The trees were opening up over the Daimler and the road widened. Eventually they pulled on to a paved road; then it was still another hour, passing nothing but logging trucks and an occasional lost vacationer, until they came to the small town of Dink, where they bought Ratchet clothes and a few groceries from the general store. The pickings were slim at the store, which was *very* general and seemed to have been stocked randomly – a few nails, a couple of cake mixes, some shower caps, a chicken in a can. Tilly held up the whole canned chicken and she and Penpen burst into hysterical giggles. "Who buys a chicken in a can?" she asked and the two of them snorted, bent double with hilarity as the sullen girl who worked the counter stared at them. They found Ratchet a small woman's swimsuit, which they decided would fit with a few safety pin adjustments. For the rest they had to make do with some boys' clothes that fit Ratchet – some ill-fitting shorts and socks and underwear – and toothbrushes and necessities. Tilly loaded up the counter and paid the girl before moving on to the post office, where they collected six months' worth of mail from their box.

Even though the postmistress knew Penpen and Tilly she made them use their key in the empty postal box before she would go in the back and give them the big bag of mail she had collected for them. "I wish you ladies would come in a mite oftener. The stuff piles up," she said. "Why, you were in town just last week. I saw you. You could have checked your mail then. You ought to get it at least as often as you're in town."

"Nonsense. It's all junk. It does make good tinder in the fireplace," said Tilly and stalked out, dragging a bag of it behind her. "Now let's go get a drink."

Penpen and Tilly took Ratchet through the thick door of the town's tavern, where she was immediately surrounded by unfamiliar smells – it was beer, dampness, cigars, woodsmoke, old wood, and the sweat of many men over many years trapped in the cool dark bar. That was why Tilly and Penpen liked it so much. That was why Ratchet liked it, though none of them knew it. It was the smell of the men. Tilly and Penpen climbed up on stools and ordered glasses of whisky for themselves and a Coke for Ratchet. They stayed for a long time, eating bar nuts, Tilly drinking many whiskies and Penpen teaching Ratchet to play pool.

"Well, well, look who's here!" came a voice, and a large man sat down and put his arm around Tilly.

18

"My goodness, Burl, your stomach is hanging over your pants!" said Tilly.

"Is that any way to speak to your own true love's son?" asked Burl thickly.

"Come on, girls," said Tilly. She threw back the rest of her whisky. "Time to go home." They spun off their stools and Ratchet made her edgy way around Burl.

"He's drunk," Tilly said tersely as soon as they got outside.

"Who was that?" Ratchet asked as they got in the car.

"Just an old fool," said Tilly, starting the car. "He thinks being born a bastard scarred him for life. As if it made any difference to anyone but him. Myrtle knew it and married him, didn't she? And as if it were my fault! My fault!"

Tilly's driving was even worse on the way home than it had been on the way to town, although Ratchet hadn't thought that possible. Three times they saw a bear coming out of the woods; one of them appeared to be lunging purposefully at the car, veering off at the last second. Ratchet gasped each time one appeared. After the third one ran off, Ratchet caught her breath and said, "They must be *really* hungry."

"I think they only do it to annoy," said Tilly and stepped on the gas, causing the car to lurch suddenly forward and Penpen's head to hit the dashboard. "Goddamn bears."

MYRTLE TROUT

It was sunset by the time they got home. Ratchet thought she would have been home sooner if she had walked and, except for the bears, wished she had.

Tilly weaved her way up the stairs and Penpen collapsed on the parlour's chaise longue. "Oh goodness," she said. "I'll make dinner after I have recovered from this peculiar dizziness that seems to come on me whenever we go into town. It'll be ten o'clock or so before I can pry these shoes off. Why don't we have dinner around then?"

Ratchet scrambled down the rocky path to the sea, where the setting sun had painted the top of the ocean cerulean and gold. The colours undulated nicely with the movement of the waves, and if she hadn't been so hungry she would have found it a very peaceful place to sit. Her mother and she didn't have many regular meals at their house either, but there was always a box of Cheerios about if she was hungry.

Ratchet stared out at the horizon. She could not stop thinking about Mrs Menuto and how she had cut off her own head, but as much as Ratchet wanted to know how she had done this, she didn't think it would be delicate to ask for the gruesome details. She sat for a long time trying to imagine methods and growing chillier and hungrier, until she heard Penpen crying, "Ratchet! Ratchet!" Penpen was racing around the grounds barefoot and tripping over lawn furniture.

Ratchet picked up her shoes from where she had taken them off to poke sea anemones with her toes and ran up the rocks. Her feet were becoming a series of small bruises and cuts, but the cold sea and stone numbed them. She did not think it could be ten o'clock already unless her sense of time had gone completely off, so she wondered what Penpen wanted.

"Ratchet!" yelled Penpen when she spied her. "Run, run, dear, it's your MOTHER on the phone!"

"*Oh!*" said Ratchet, racing into the house. Penpen came huffing and puffing behind Ratchet and showed her where to find the phone.

"*Hello!*" said Ratchet quickly, worried that her mother had already hung up, and she had lost her chance.

"Don't shout, Ratchet. I just called to see if you'd arrived," said Henriette.

"Yes, I'm fine," Ratchet said.

"Well, of course you're fine. Listen, the last time you tidied, what did you do with my new black riding gloves?"

"I put them in the coat closet, in the pocket of your riding jacket."

21

"Oh, for heaven's sakes. No wonder I couldn't find them. Next time, do you mind putting them someplace in plain sight?"

"OK," answered Ratchet. At the sound of her mother's voice, her stomach churned with homesickness.

"I know Tilly is going to want to talk to me, but it's bad enough I had to listen to all of Penpen's drivel, so tell her I had to go to an appointment or something and didn't have time to talk. Penpen says that they're not as well as they used to be, but they were always complaining about something."

"OK."

"And, Ratchet, keep That Thing covered."

"I am." Ratchet turned her back to Penpen, who was in the kitchen, and whispered, "Mom, how long am I staying here?"

"I told you you were staying the whole summer, so don't worry, no one is going to whisk you away just when you're having fun. Oops, time for *Wheel of Fortune*," said Henriette and hung up.

"Dinner is almost ready," said Penpen when Ratchet put down the receiver. "I suddenly remembered that girls get very hungry, so I threw something together and I woke Tilly up. She should be down soon."

Ratchet helped Penpen put things on the table. Tilly came into the dining room, looking drawn, as if sleep brought to the edge of extinction what life remained in that old body. As she slowly woke up, a flickering light reappeared within her like the dawn.

"We're having creamed chicken," said Penpen, ladling some on to Ratchet's plate. "I'm sorry. It's not very inspired."

Ratchet started. She had spent so much time thinking about creamed chicken it was as if she had willed Penpen to make it.

Ratchet looked around the big old wood-panelled dining room with its good china and the slow, deliberate movements of her aunts. It was so late and she was so tired that she just wanted the meal to be eaten and over, but Tilly put her napkin on her lap and asked Ratchet to say grace. Ratchet froze. She didn't know a grace. The closest she could come was "Thank God for the Hunt Club."

"Perhaps, Tilly," said Penpen, "I should say a Buddhist metta prayer. I just recently came across one in Father's library that goes, 'May all beings be happy, content, and fulfilled. May all beings be healed and whole. . .'"

Tilly, who had lifted her fork loaded with chicken, which was the moment Ratchet had waited for, put it down suddenly, and Ratchet was filled with despair, thinking she would have to hear a longer prayer, but Tilly said, "You know what? I forgot to milk the cow."

Penpen put her fork down. "Oh, Tilly, you didn't?"

Ratchet put her fork down, too. Would they never get this food to their lips?

"I did," said Tilly wearily. "The cream sauce reminded me."

"Well, Tilly, if the cow has exploded while we were in town, it is on your head."

"I'll go see to it now," said Tilly, getting up uncertainly from the table and walking stooped over, dragging one foot slightly, as she made her way to the hall to grab her shawl and a flashlight. "You two go ahead and eat!" she shouted over her shoulder.

"She can't handle that old cow alone at this hour," muttered Penpen, getting up to follow her. Ratchet got up, too, but took a surreptitious mouthful of chicken before joining Penpen, who was trailing Tilly out to the barn. From behind, Tilly looked like a troll.

"She's tired," whispered Penpen. "And when she's tired she has a hard time standing upright. It's her back. I think the discs in her spine wander off in different directions. It's as if the mortar has loosened. Dr Richardson pokes it back into place sometimes. It helps for a while, but at our age nothing helps for ever except the final help, if you know what I mean."

The moon was bright and a thousand stars were in the sky. They seemed to talk a lot about dying, thought Ratchet. Just looking at them made Ratchet think of death. It didn't seem so terrible out on this big chunk of land surrounded by the sky and the ocean and the forest. On a starry night like this it seemed at worst a change of venue. Nevertheless, Ratchet didn't want anyone dying tonight. They'd never get to the creamed chicken.

In the barn Tilly was very, very slow, each movement maddeningly deliberate and careful as if she had to concentrate on the individual action of each of her muscles in order to get them to work. Ratchet was so desperate to speed things along and get back to dinner that she lost her shyness and ran to get Tilly the things she needed, urging her just to point and let her fetch because she could do it so much faster: anything, anything to move them closer to dinner. When Tilly began to milk, it was an agony of suspended animation, a slow pull of a teat, a rest, another slow pull.

"I think I could do that!" Ratchet finally said in exasperation, knowing that if Tilly milked, they'd be there all night. "Could I try?"

"Don't pull too hard," said Tilly, getting creakily up.

"I won't."

24

"And don't annoy the cow," said Tilly.

"She's not going to annoy this old cow," said Penpen, who was holding the cow's neck. "This old cow just wants to be milked and left alone."

Ratchet sat down at the milking stool. The feel of the teat made her shudder and she didn't get anything at first, but then as the milk came down, she was surprised by the rush of excitement she felt. She liked the earthy smell of the cow and its acceptance of her. She almost felt like leaning her head forward against it, but she couldn't do this with Penpen and Tilly watching.

Ratchet worked quickly once she got the hang of it, and when the pail was full she was ready to go back and eat, but Tilly said, "Now we have to take it over to the cream separator."

"Why don't you go inside and finish your dinner?" said Penpen. "It's going to be a while for us. We have more chores in the barn."

It seemed unfair to eat before they did, so Ratchet stayed and helped, lifting things that were difficult for them. Ratchet was amazed at all they could do when she saw how physically demanding it was, hauling bales of hay down. Penpen did more than Tilly, but Ratchet thought it remarkable that either one could do so much at their age. By the time they had finished, Ratchet had hay in her hair and all down her front, her hands were nicked from trying to remove the twine that bound the hay bales so tightly, she could smell the cow on herself, and she wasn't even hungry any more, she was so tired. This kind of tiredness was new to her, and when they finally returned to the dining room table, she ate her dinner automatically and went up to bed exhausted.

Melissa Public Library
Melissa, Texas

In the morning Ratchet woke up at sunrise when the rooster crowed. She waited on the porch for Tilly, but when she didn't come, Ratchet went to the barn and milked the cow herself, fed it, and cleaned out its stall before going back to the house.

Penpen was taking last night's cloth off the table when Ratchet came in. Tilly had knocked over her sherry during dinner while they had been cramming down creamed chicken, and no one had had the energy to do anything about it. After dinner they had simply gone upstairs, leaving the dirty dishes and spills.

"It was our mother's," said Penpen as Ratchet helped her gather up the huge cloth that covered the ten-foot table. "She had two good cloths. This one and a maroon one she used when she killed herself. To catch the drippings."

"By drippings you mean. . ."

"She didn't want to make a mess." Penpen hustled off and returned with porridge. "Although she did. What she didn't count on was that it would bounce."

"What?" asked Ratchet.

"The head. Would you like to go for a swim?"

Ratchet opened her mouth but couldn't think of anything to say, so she went upstairs and put on her swimsuit and then had two horrible thoughts that drove the vision of a bouncing head out of her mind. One was that she didn't know how to swim. The second was that the swimsuit would reveal That Thing. She put a T-shirt over the swimsuit. She would just leave the T-shirt on while she swam. Then she realized that That Thing would be visible through a wet T-shirt, so she put a cardigan on over that. They might think

Melissa Public Library
Melissa, Texas

it was queer, but it was better than being exposed. This taken care of, she went back to wondering where the head had bounced. When the phone rang, it was so startling it was like a visitor from another planet.

"Ratchet!" called Penpen. "It's for you again!"

Ratchet ran downstairs.

"The only two calls we've had in six months!" drawled Tilly from her chair, where she was very slowly eating her breakfast. "And they're both for her. I told you this was what it would be like having a teenager in the house. I told you the phone would never stop ringing!"

"It's Henriette," hissed Penpen.

"That woman—" began Tilly, but Penpen shoved a bowl of raspberries at her, saying, "Look, Tilly, they've all spoiled."

"Well, they always spoil," said Tilly cantankerously. "Because you always pick too many and we don't can them. Before you know it, it's going to be blueberry time. Now, you don't see any spoiled blueberries, do you? No. And do you know why? Because we can them."

"Oh dear, Tilly," said Penpen. "I just don't know about this year. Are we up to dealing with all those berries? Should we bring in Myrtle?"

"We never should have asked Myrtle in the first place. Now we have to put up with her whenever she wants to say hello. It opens a whole can of worms when you go around making contact with people. I don't know why we bothered with help to begin with. I don't know why we didn't do it all ourselves."

"Everyone needs help during the canning season," said Penpen.

Tilly made a face and continued to chew the same mouthful she had been working on for the last ten minutes. It was hard for her very old jaws and the working parts of her mouth to mush up and process food, but time, she often said, was what you spent it on, and she enjoyed her meals. When she remembered to take them.

"Ratchet!" said Henriette sharply.

Ratchet was standing mutely breathing into the receiver, riveted by Penpen and Tilly's conversation.

"Hi, Mom," she said, starting.

"I looked into the cost of shipping your things, and it's just exorbitant. It's ridiculous. Penpen said I should send them, but I'm not going to do it."

"Penpen and Tilly bought me some things," Ratchet said.

"Without even asking me? I suppose they want me to pay for those, too. Well, they'll have to send me receipts. What did you get? Something you can wear year round, I hope."

"We got some shorts and T-shirts and a swimsuit."

"You're not going swimming, are you?" barked Henriette.

"No," Ratchet lied.

"You can't wear a swimsuit. Why did you let them buy you a swimsuit?"

"I couldn't say no without explaining," Ratchet whispered.

"Well, they can just try to send me the bill for that one," said Henriette and hung up.

"My mother said if you sent her the receipt for the clothes she would send you a cheque," Ratchet said.

Tilly looked up from her breakfast and snorted. "A receipt!

Come on down to the beach, Ratchet." They went out into the bright sunshine and down the steep cliffside path.

Ratchet waded in up to her knees behind Tilly and Penpen, who were walking purposefully into the water. "I don't know how to swim," she said.

"I can teach you," said Tilly. She eyed Ratchet's cardigan. "First you have to get wet."

"I don't think I'm ready for this," Ratchet said and waded along the shore. It sounded lame even to her. Tilly looked as if she was about to demand to know just what Ratchet meant by this, when a wave nearly knocked Ratchet over, giving her an excuse to go sit on the rocks while Penpen and Tilly swam back and forth in waist-deep water – their only concession to age. Then they heard someone call "HELLOOO" from the cliff top.

"Oh God, it's Myrtle," hissed Tilly, treading water and squinting up the hill.

"Hello, Myrtle!" called Penpen, smiling and waving from the sea.

"Hello, hello, you queer Menutos," Myrtle muttered as she made her slow, uncertain way down the rocky path.

Tilly assumed a martyred expression and walked slowly from the water, grabbing a towel to dry herself off and shake water out of her ear. Penpen got out and settled herself comfortably in the sun to dry like a fat old wrinkled walrus.

"Ratchet, this is Mrs Trout. You've already met her husband, Burl, at the tavern. Myrtle, this is our relative from Florida, Ratchet Clark."

"Well, I wondered what you two old things were doing with a

29

child. Burl said you'd somehow acquired one. I said to myself that that child didn't just walk in. It would have been eaten by the bears. It isn't Henriette's daughter, is it, Tilly?"

"Well, of course she is, Myrtle," said Tilly.

"Your mother—" began Myrtle, turning to Ratchet.

"Would you like something to eat?" interrupted Penpen.

"We haven't taught Ratchet how to swim yet," said Tilly. She wasn't going to let old Myrtle Trout lumber in and throw her weight around. It was bad enough they had to deal with her during the canning season.

"Well, if you'll forgive my stupidity—" began Myrtle.

"But of course," said Penpen.

"Isn't Florida on a nice warm ocean of its own?" Myrtle asked Ratchet.

"Yes," said Ratchet.

"With bathing beaches?"

"Yes," said Ratchet.

"Then how come you don't know how to swim?"

"Just what are you doing here anyhow, Myrtle?" asked Tilly.

"Oh. Well, Tilly, I've brought you this basket of sewing things." Myrtle held it out to Tilly and then changed her mind when she saw how wet she was. She held it out to Penpen next, but pulled it back when she realized that Penpen was twice as wet because there was twice as much of her. Finally she handed it to Ratchet, although it was clear that she wasn't satisfied with this solution either, yet didn't want to have to carry it back up that rocky path herself. Then she took their pile of towels and clothes and scooted the lot about a foot to the right, saying, "Now, Penpen, I'd move this stuff a few inches so that the towels are on the rocks and can dry out better so."

"I don't know why you're giving us those sewing things," said Tilly. "We don't sew. We haven't sewn for years."

"Yes, I know that, Tilly Menuto. That's why I brought you these things." Myrtle gave Ratchet a big smile as if to say, Aren't your aunts silly? "You see, everyone in town is making a great big quilt to auction off at Christmas to raise money for the volunteer fire department, which will have to come bail you out if this firetrap of yours ever spontaneously combusts. And I recall people saying that your father was a member many many years ago when the department was first being formed. Wasn't he, Penpen? Now, you need to make a square at least twelve inches by twelve inches. Any pattern you like. We're putting it together as a crazy quilt and we're all signing our pieces. It will be a nice historical object, as well as functional. Some people are making more than one square, not that I said I expected the two of you to. We almost forgot you completely out here alone in the woods, but I said I thought you'd like to be included in such a historical kind of occasion. Nobody wanted to be the one to drive out all this way here, so you nearly weren't; however, I volunteered on account of Burl's father being married to you, Tilly. I thought you'd feel obligated to do what you could for Burl's volunteer fire department because even though he's technically no relation, you know that if it wasn't for you he wouldn't be illegitimate and that's just a fact."

"Oh God, not again!" said Tilly.

"Now, I've included a book of quilt patterns in case you can't think of any of your own," Myrtle went on implacably as if Tilly hadn't spoken. "Of course, I'll have to charge you for the fabric and thread even if you don't use it all, but I have lent you the scissors and needle free of charge."

"That's very kind of you," said Tilly acidly. "Ratchet, take off that sweater and T-shirt and come in the water and learn to swim."

"I really don't want to learn," Ratchet said, panicking because she thought they had successfully avoided that subject.

"Nonsense," said Tilly. "You'll enjoy it."

"I don't think so," Ratchet said quietly to herself. She kept her sweater on and edged her way into the waves.

"Take off your things, dear!" called Penpen, thinking she had forgotten to remove them.

"I'm chilly," Ratchet said, although the sun was beating down heavily on them.

"There's something wrong with that child," said Myrtle conversationally to Penpen. "To be chilly in weather like this? Henriette didn't send her because she's dying, did she?"

"Well, not that I know. . ." said Penpen absently, wondering if she should offer Myrtle some tea. She was getting hungry.

"Don't be silly. You'll warm up in seconds once you get moving," said Tilly. "Those wet clothes are going to twist all around you and make it hard to swim."

"I don't mind," said Ratchet.

"Well, this is a lot of nonsense," said Myrtle, going to her sewing basket. Ratchet had her back to the shore and didn't see Myrtle walking toward her and couldn't hear her over the waves and wasn't thinking anyhow, frozen with the fear of Tilly trying to get her to remove her sweater. Nobody had ever seen That Thing except her mother and some medical people. So she wasn't aware that Myrtle was right behind her until with six fast long snips she had cut the cardigan and T-shirt right down the back and, grabbing the two sides, ripped them off Ratchet's arms in one vicious yank. And there Ratchet stood in nothing but her swimsuit.

"Well, Lord in heaven, what's that thing on the child's shoulder blade?" asked Myrtle.

THE GRAVES

"My God, Myrtle Trout!" said Tilly. "Imagine ruining a dollar ninety-eight T-shirt like that. Not to mention the only sweater this child has here. Damn it, Myrtle!"

"Nonsense, Tilly Menuto. You shouldn't let a child talk back to you like that. Won't take off her things to learn to swim! What pap! I showed you the way to deal with such matters, is all. Having reared twelve children of my own, I hope I have a little experience in the matter."

"Don't you think you could have been more tactful, dear?" asked Penpen, wringing her hands. She hated to have Tilly riled. Tilly had a temper of her own.

"I'm telling you, once you start that, you leave the floodgates open. Wide open. Someday this child will be a teenager and then where will you be?"

"What do you mean someday? She's already a teenager," said Tilly.

Myrtle looked Ratchet up and down. "Well, I never would have guessed. She looks about ten to me. What's the matter with her? I mean besides that thing on her shoulder blade."

Ratchet squatted under the water.

"Honestly, Myrtle, will you go home?" said Tilly. "At least you're in the water now, Ratchet." Tilly and Ratchet walked out deeper until they were in neck-deep water. Tilly turned her back on Myrtle and began to demonstrate the flutter kick as if nothing had happened.

"You'll have trouble with that child, treating her like a princess," called Myrtle.

"Well, I was going to ask you for tea, but perhaps some other time would be best." Penpen flitted about, trying to escort Myrtle back up the path. She and Tilly never left each other alone on the beach, but now Ratchet was there.

"You're going to have trouble with that girl," Myrtle said again to Penpen, since Tilly wouldn't listen.

"Oh, I don't think . . . she's only here for the summer."

"Long enough, trust me. Well, you get to work on that square."

"Yes, Myrtle."

"And take care of my good scissors."

"Yes, Myrtle."

"They're made of real nickel."

"Really?"

"That's used in alloys, you know."

"I have no idea what you're talking about," said Penpen pleasantly. "Do say hello to Burl for us."

"Humph," said Myrtle and climbed slowly up the path with

Penpen trailing a few feet behind. Halfway up, Myrtle fell backward on to a sharply pointed boulder. She sat on it like an eraser on the end of a pencil. Ratchet saw Penpen waiting for Myrtle to wiggle off and the battle on Penpen's face as she tried not to be pleased. Myrtle unstuck herself and lumbered the rest of the way up the hill. When she got to her car, she looked at the garden sundial and said, "Penpen Menuto, I'd move that old sundial a few inches to the right if I were you, or that big tree is going to start casting its shadow on it once it's grown a foot or so. Just a few inches to the right. That ought to do it." Nodding with satisfaction, she got in her car and drove off, her head moving from side to side, looking for bears.

Tilly finished the swimming lesson. Ratchet couldn't tell if she was ignoring That Thing or just wasn't noticing it, but she didn't mention it and her eyes never strayed there. Afterward Ratchet tried to put the two parts of her sweater and T-shirt on, but they fell open at the back. Penpen had returned to the beach to finish sunning, and they all climbed the path to the house together.

"I'm so angry at that Myrtle Trout," muttered Tilly all the way up. "I'm so mad I can hardly speak. Ruining a good sweater like that. I need lunch, Penpen. I need a good hearty lunch. Why don't you make chilli?"

"We ought to have something like chowder that uses up all this morning's cream. *Ratchet* remembered to milk the cow."

"All right. Chowder, chilli, it's all the same to me," said Tilly. "Damn woman!" She could be heard muttering all the way upstairs, "Damn, damn woman."

But lunch wasn't ever eaten because after Penpen made the chowder, she waited for Tilly, and Tilly went up to change and forgot what she was about, lay down for a moment, and, tired out from the morning's swim, fell asleep the rest of the afternoon. Sleep, Tilly said, came to the old like the transition, the hallway between life and death. You needed less food and wandered more through the corridors of dreams. Sometimes she met her mother there, and others. Time seemed to lose meaning, your past and your present and your future all coming together somehow, so that sometimes you couldn't keep anyone or their time with you straight. The sequence didn't seem so important somehow anyway. It was as if it were all being played out at once until you figured it out. Borrowing from the future, trying to figure out what you missed in the past, going through passageways where the living and the dead convened.

Penpen went, as she did every afternoon, to work in the Menutos' kitchen garden, where, distracted by the weeds, she forgot lunch altogether. Ratchet came out to sit on a bench and let her hair dry in the sun, watching Penpen pick off dead buds and thin things and do other gardening tasks Ratchet didn't understand. Tilly and Penpen referred to it as their kitchen garden, but it was really Penpen's. She loved gardening. They depended on the vegetables from it, but even if they hadn't Penpen would have been out there every day, listening to bees buzz, watching things grow. Penpen said that living things were all critical mass, the definition of critical mass being the amount of fissionable material required to sustain a chain reaction. She tossed some weeds on the compost and said that people didn't like to see things rotting in the garden but there had to be all things to be growth. She told Ratchet this over and over, and the things that someone repeats to you over and over you tend to remember. It wasn't until dinner time that Tilly finally wandered downstairs and they got around to the chowder.

The big grandfather clock in the hall was striking seven when they sat at the table. Tilly had come in wearing a housedress, slippers, and nylons. Through her nylons Ratchet could see big bruises. Tilly spied her gaping and said, "That's your doing. That's where you kicked me underwater when you were trying to flutter-kick."

Ratchet put her hand to her mouth. She hadn't tried to kick Tilly, but she had kept her legs as low as she could because she wanted to keep her shoulders underwater.

"Oh, don't worry so. At our age, flesh is like rotting fruit. We get bruises for no reason. I can't feel a thing. It's as if this flesh is already dead. It's just this thing humming inside me, keeping me going. What's for dinner?"

Penpen came out carrying a big tureen of chowder. There was already a basket of crackers on the table. Ratchet decided to eat until bursting in case meals always landed as randomly as they had since she arrived. She was on her fourth bowl of chowder when she looked up and said to Tilly, "I didn't know you had been married." It just popped into her head, and she was so full after being so hungry that it made her a little stupid and she didn't stop to think first. Then she was embarrassed because it sounded like prying.

Penpen smiled at her. "It isn't a secret."

"It was a brief but wholly satisfying marriage," said Tilly. "At any rate, I never wanted to do it again. Penpen, bring on the cheese. I acquired the cheese habit when I was sixteen and Father took us for the grand tour. A year in Europe. That's what you did back when we were young if your family had money. Your parents took you for the grand tour. Smarten you up. Give you a few Continental pretensions. And what I came back with was the idea of cheese for dessert. Instead of sweet things, goopy pies, towering cakes, things Cook made for afters. So now I try to keep a variety of cheese on hand. I talked that fool who owns the general store in Dink into stocking some decent cheeses, and we were both astounded when he said they could hardly keep them in stock. They're surprisingly popular even with folks you wouldn't think could afford them. So when we go in for supplies once a month or so we get a good Stilton and some Camembert and some Port Salut and make like mice. We laid in a big supply the week before you came. In anticipation. In case you were a cheese person. Are you a cheese person? Penpen, bring the cheese. I have to rest my legs."

"I don't know if I'm a cheese person. I'm sorry about the bruises," Ratchet said because she couldn't stop thinking about Tilly's black-and-blue legs.

"Think nothing of it," said Tilly. "I have eaten and I feel a world of difference. Nothing like some food, eh, Ratchet?"

Ratchet couldn't agree more. She hoped Tilly would note what a difference a meal made and perhaps remember them with a little more regularity. Penpen, who had left to make coffee, returned with cheese, and Tilly cut it into teensy tinsy pieces to make it last longer.

She was, it turned out, a wee bit stingy with her cheese supply, cutting herself big chunks and the merest nibbles for Penpen and Ratchet.

"Now, where were we? Oh yes." Tilly rolled some Stilton around on her tongue. "What this Stilton needs is a good port. Penpen, get out the port and pour me a little glass, please."

Penpen walked over to the mahogany liquor cabinet, bent down, and opened it with the tiny silver key that they always used. There were no longer servants about to steal the port, but Penpen had loved using the tiny silver key since she was a child of eight and was first allowed to do so, and she wasn't about to stop now that she could use it all the time. "Tilly, dear, there is no more port."

"No port?" asked Tilly.

Penpen made a sad face and from her bent-over position held up the empty port bottle for Tilly to see.

"Well, make it rum, then," said Tilly. "So, it all began when—"

"Tilly, dear, I do so hate to keep interrupting, but the rum's gone, too."

"What exactly do we have, Penpen?" asked Tilly, putting the flat of her hands on the top of the table to push herself into a half-rising position and peer down toward the liquor cabinet. "You might have noticed the diminishing supply before we went into town."

"Well, let's see, we have some very nasty-looking Bailey's Irish Cream and a little Cointreau."

"Go for the Cointreau. I'll switch to Camembert. OK, we had just gotten back from our grand tour of Europe. I was seventeen. Thank you, Penpen," said Tilly as Penpen set a liqueur glass in front of her.

"We got these Venetian handblown glasses on the grand tour, Ratchet," said Penpen. "Aren't they nice?"

"Very," Ratchet said.

"Can I offer you a Cointreau?" asked Tilly.

"No, thank you," said Ratchet.

"Drambuie? Did you say we had Drambuie?" asked Tilly.

"Bailey's Irish Cream. And it looks nasty," said Penpen.

"Liquor doesn't go nasty," said Tilly. "That's the good thing about liquor. Very well, then, a sherry perhaps."

"We haven't any sherry left," said Penpen. "Cooking sherry maybe."

"I don't think she'd like cooking sherry," said Tilly.

"It's rather salty," said Penpen.

"Do you like salty things, Ratchet?" asked Tilly.

"I'm fine, really," said Ratchet.

"OK, well, we'd gotten back from the grand tour," said Tilly. "I wandered around the property, which was much as it is today, only the grounds were nicer and Mother's gardens were better kept up because we had gardeners, you see. Anyhow, nice as they were, and even though I could always fill my days with swimming and sunning, after the excitement of Europe, two weeks here with nothing much to do and I was bored silly."

"I wasn't bored because I'd just discovered Jane Austen, so I spent that whole summer in the hammock reading all of Jane Austen, and after Jane Austen, Proust, which I didn't enjoy so much but there was more of it," said Penpen.

"Yes, people think twins are going to be like, well, twins, but we are as different as chalk and cheese. I recall her, slouched in that hammock, no help at all with the wedding. Until that summer we'd always gone into town together with Cook to do the weekly shopping. Father didn't pay much attention to what we did; we were always being cared for by one servant or another. The day Mother died, Cook took us into town with her where she had to get food for the funeral. She left us in the tavern while she shopped, setting us on two barstools and giving us each a stiff whisky. We'd been coming in with Cook ever since. We'd go into the tavern, sit on a stool, and have six or seven shots of whisky while Cook was buying groceries, filling the car, and gossiping with friends. It's just something we did, a diversion, and I, for one, looked forward to it. The summer we got back from the grand tour I wanted to go back to hanging out at the tavern when Cook went into town, but Penpen had discovered Proust. She stopped going along with me because she was always reading, reading, reading."

"Proust is very engrossing," said Penpen.

"Anyhow, I started going alone, but one day Cook and I got back and Father saw me stumble out of the Daimler and was livid. Just livid. He charged about saying that now that I was a young woman, now that I had come out – and the grand tour for someone living in the woods is as out as you can get – he expected me to stay on the property. Both me and Penpen. Well, I began to see why Mother chopped off her own head. She wasn't just going to put an end to the boredom, she was going to do it in the way that offered the most entertainment value. I went up to Penpen, who was reading, of course, and said, 'We gotta get out of here before it's too late. That man is going to bury us alive.'

"Penpen said, 'Who? Father?' as if she didn't have a brain in her head."

"But really I was just completely engrossed in my book. And unlike Tilly, after all that fuss in Europe I was more than happy to be at home reading and puttering in the garden, so Father's little tantrums passed right over my head," said Penpen.

" 'Yes, of course Father! He means to bury us here!' I said.

"And Penpen, without taking her eyes off the page, said, 'I know. In two plots right next to Mother's.'

" '*What?*' I roared, because of course I hadn't meant it literally. And before Penpen could answer, I charged off into the family cemetery and there I saw two headstones to the right of Mother's for me and Penpen and the one to the left of Mother that Father had erected for himself. 'Oh, now really, he's gone too far this time,' I muttered frantically to myself. Because deciding where someone was going to be buried was just a little too pushy. I mean, suppose I had other plans? Suppose I planned to be halfway around the globe by the time I died? I was infuriated and I felt suddenly as if I couldn't breathe and I was mad as a hornet because at the tavern the bartender had told me that Lilla Vanilla was getting married."

TILLY'S BRIEF BUT ODDLY SATISFYING MARRIAGE

Penpen and Ratchet sat expectantly looking at the wispy crown of Tilly's head because she had pushed her liqueur glass away and put her forehead down on the table, to take a break, or so they thought, but after a while it became apparent by her snores that she was out like a light. So they woke her gently and helped her up to bed and then went to bed themselves, Ratchet wondering who in the world Lilla Vanilla was.

The next morning after milking, Ratchet found Tilly at the breakfast table eating mouldering raspberries and ready to pick up the thread of her story as if no time had passed at all.

"Lilla Vanilla was a lumberjack's daughter. Her real name was Lilla, but everyone called her Lilla Vanilla because her skin was so milky white. She bleached it with buttermilk all summer, so that she always had a slightly sour smell. I was surprised that anyone who got in noseshot would want to keep Lilla at close quarters. But later

I found out that all the men wanted Lilla. She was so well wanted that she was pregnant, or as we used to call it, in a pickle, although only Lilla's father was supposed to know that. Her mother was dead, same as ours.

"Lilla didn't know which of her many suitors was the father. Her father didn't much care either. After all, did it really matter whose genetic foibles were bouncing around in there? His idea was to get a list of possibles from her, choose the pick of the litter, and march him up the aisle. He decided that the banker's son had the most possibilities, and charged over there to tell him what was going to happen to him if he didn't make an honest woman out of Lilla. Which was certainly closing the barn door . . . but I mustn't editorialize. Now, the banker's son was no great prize himself, was he, Penpen?"

"He wouldn't have been my choice," said Penpen, who had brought in some oatmeal and was picking through the berries looking for a few good ones.

"Being a series of hairy moles like some kind of giant connect-the-dot game in the flesh. Men around this part of Maine outnumbered the women at least two to one, what with all the lumberjacks, so mating was always a problem for the men, and the banker's son was more than happy to get Lilla because despite her sour-milk smell she did have undeniably nice skin and wasn't too hard to look at generally, and besides when someone's poking you in the stomach with a rake handle, which is the weapon Lilla's father had chosen (oddly, since he owned two hunting rifles), you might as well try to be accommodating.

"So Lilla's dad was able to go back and tell Lilla that her problem had been solved and they could just march over to the justice of the peace the next day and get it over with.

" 'But, Daaaaaady,' Lilla bawled, 'I want a *real* wedding with a *real* dress and a *real* ring and a *real* engagement and. . .' Just thinking about it calmed her down, and she went to her bedroom to get her list: 'a church, flowers, a reception, bridesmaids, dresses, engraved invitations, showers, honeymoon. . .'

"Lilla's father, who was pacing around, tried to explain that such a wedding for a woman in Lilla's delicate condition was unseemly. But she didn't care. She cried and cried and finally pulled out all the stops and dragged out her dead mother, whom she'd been careful never to use before, saving her for just such an occasion, and said that if her *mother* had been alive, *she* would have given her daughter a proper wedding. *She* would have understood. *She* would have wanted it *herself*!

"That did it because Lilla's father's Achilles' heel ever since his wife died when Lilla was six was his secret fear that he was not equipped to raise a daughter alone. And sure enough, here she was pregnant. And claiming that he didn't know the first thing about throwing a wedding, which was true enough. So, being completely befuddled and scared to death, he raised one eyebrow and said, 'Now, I'm not saying I'm doing this here thing you want and I'm not saying I'm not, but supposing I did, what is it you say you need?'

"And so she continued to read her list. She needs a chauffeur-driven limousine, and an announcement in the paper – not *just* the local paper. . .

"He couldn't listen to any more, it was making him dizzy, so he said, 'Well, fine, fine, fine, but you gotta do it *soon*, Lilla, before, you know, before it becomes *apparent*, because I won't have us disgraced.'

" 'Well,' said Lilla, throwing her hands up in the air, 'there goes the engagement.'

"She bit on a knuckle and said that they'd better get busy because they'd have to cram all that engagement *stuff* into the next couple of weeks even if there wasn't going to be an engagement. The way she figured it, you shouldn't have to have an engagement to get the engagement *stuff*. Now go away, she barked, completely recovered from the agonies of a moment ago, she had plans to make. Plans!

"Lilla went into Dairy for things, getting invitations printed and the dress altered and the cake ordered. Of course, it was all so rushed that it was cheaper and more ready-made than she'd have liked. Her father thought it was maybe a bit unseemly that she hadn't even taken any time out to have a little quiet remorseful period. But no, it's tulle and marzipan ho!

" 'God knows where she learned about things like this,' said her father one night in the tavern, wiping sweat off his brow after another considerable session with Lilla from which he'd only just escaped. He walked out when she got to the part about favours for the guests. 'I don't know nothing about things like this,' he went on plaintively to anyone in the bar who would listen. 'But it sounds fishy to me. *Us* giving *them* presents. I thought it was supposed to be the other way around. We're *feeding* them, aren't we? How do I know she's not making this stuff up? Tents and rehearsals and

47

garters, taking your undergarments off and throwing them about! Bridesmaid presents! Are there no end to the presents? Every day it's something new. This evening,' he went on despairingly, 'it was shrimp remoulade. Now, I ask you, whoever heard of such a thing? I can't barely pronounce it. I wish to God there was someone I could hire to listen to her because I can't do it no more.'

"His prayers were answered because an enterprising young waitress named Thelma came out from behind the bar, threw down her bar towel, and said, 'I'll do it! I'll tell you what these fancy ladies in big cities have, Clyde, because I was reading about it in *Ladies' Home Journal*. They got wedding planners. That's someone who comes in and plans the whole shebang and gets paid for doing it so folks like you just have to show up and look pretty. You pay me what I'll lose in tips and wages for the next couple of weeks and I'll take it on.'

" 'You're hired,' said Lilla's father. 'And I hope you got strong ears. Now give me another one of them beers.'

"Lilla's wedding was the biggest thing to hit Dink since a logger rolled his truck. It wiped out Clyde's bank account but also any residual guilt he had about not knowing how to raise a girl and any guilt he had about mistakes he might have unconsciously made along the way. It was the best entertainment the women in Dink had had in years and they fell on it like flies on honey. And every other girl in town was green with envy even though Lilla never could keep her mouth shut, so they all knew why she was headed for that blissful state."

Penpen got up and got herself another bowl of oatmeal and

called through the open kitchen door, "All this was happening at the time Tilly was scouting around for a way to alleviate her boredom whenever she went into town with Cook."

"Yes, yes, I'm getting to that, Penpen. I'm just explaining what led up to it," said Tilly.

"Ah," said Penpen, coming in with a bowl brimming with cream. Tilly whispered to Ratchet that Penpen ate oatmeal mostly as a vehicle for the cream.

"So anyhow, Ratchet, the bartender brought me up to date on Lilla and it occurred to me that if I could get myself married, why that'd keep me entertained for at least a year or two. Then around my sixth or seventh whisky, Burl came into the bar and I said, 'Burl, you and me ought to get married.' And he said to me, 'OK, just let me have one more beer first.' "

Ratchet had to stop the story at this point because she was getting confused. "You mean that guy we met at the tavern – Burl – was your husband?"

"No, no," said Tilly. "That was Burl's son, Burl Junior. The Burl I married is taking a dirt bath."

"Myrtle Trout is Burl Junior's wife," said Penpen helpfully.

"Burl Senior's second wife (sort of) ended up being Thelma the waitress, but that doesn't come into the story until later. She's long gone, too." Tilly put both palms flat on the table with a smack. "God, Penpen! My whole cast of characters is dead and their children are all pretty ancient. Burl Junior is about sixty, can you imagine? And little Myrtle. How long has it been since she's been *little* Myrtle? What a long time since I thought of her as anything other than the type of thing you'd smear on a microscope slide."

"Tell her about the wedding," said Penpen.

Tilly had had several glasses of Cointreau with her cereal. The liqueur glass was tiny, but even so they added up and her eyes were beginning to go out of focus. "The wedding? Now, wasn't that the most romantic thing, Penpen? Wasn't that so beautiful?"

"It sure was," said Penpen.

"Right up to the vows," said Tilly. Then she sank in her chair and her head flopped back as if her neck were made of rubber. "Whew, what a lucky break that was. I mean, the vows. Burl and I decided to tie the knot and I came home from the tavern to tell Father and he was pretty good with it although he said he didn't like the idea of a big wedding. Tacky. Big weddings were very low-class. They were for the nouveaux riches to show off their worldly goods and they devalued women by treating them like chattel. And also the stock market had been a bit wonky, so we couldn't afford one. How about a small private ceremony and an ocean crossing, although, come to think of it, we couldn't afford Europe either.

" 'Well, where are we going to cross *to*?' I asked. 'Greenland?' So I ended up like Lilla Vanilla, storming around, although, of course, I didn't cry because I never cry. I couldn't believe he didn't get that the whole point was to spend a couple of years planning the thing. And also, of course, if we were going to do it we would have to outshine Lilla Vanilla. 'You don't want me having some rotten old thing with folding chairs and an accordion band like Lilla Vanilla.'

"He looked horrified even though he didn't know who Lilla Vanilla was, but the words 'accordion band' struck terror in his heart and he asked me how long we had to get ready for this thing and I said, oh, two, three years, and he heaved a sigh of relief, figuring he'd be back in the old financial saddle by then.

"So I began my own trips into Dink and Dairy and Delta to find caterers and champagne and such. Thelma offered to be my wedding planner, too, but I said no because, of course, the whole point was to do the planning myself, and it ticked her off, so she went around telling everyone that I planned to serve beer and doughnuts.

"When I could, I pried Penpen's nose out of her book and took her in for fittings for her bridesmaid dress because, of course, Penpen was to be the only attendant. Our tutor, Miss Greengage, said that people didn't seem to figure real big in my wedding but she was probably sour because, to be honest, I wasn't really even planning on inviting her. She'd long ago stopped tutoring us. I don't even know why Father kept her around. Probably because he'd forgotten what her specific job was. He was just used to her face, so he kind of absent-mindedly kept her on the payroll. Occasionally she'd try to cram a few Latin verbs down our throats."

"But they got stuck," said Penpen.

"How could we concentrate on Latin verbs when we had a wedding?"

"And Proust," said Penpen.

"Anyhow, toward the end of the two years I ran out of things to plan and buy and about the only thing left was to pick our vows. This was a bit of a puzzler because we weren't with any particular church. Father always said grace at dinner but in the same way he kept Miss Greengage on the payroll, without any real idea why he was doing it. Burl didn't come from churchgoers either. Because we weren't affiliated with any special churches, so that there was nothing we *had* to use, I figured we'd each choose our own vows. Burl said he didn't know where to find vows, so I told him to make something up. Unbeknownst to me, he went and got help from the guy the lumber company brought in to preach to the men. The lumber company couldn't afford a full-time minister's salary, so what they ended up with was this ex-convict who, for three meals a day, gave inspirational pep talks based on a self-esteem course he had been forced to take before they would parole him. But, as I say, I didn't know this at the time. I was busy digging up my own vows.

"I started by rooting through the devotional part of Father's library and I was amazed at all the literature available for wedding vows. At first I thought I'd use the Book of Common Prayer, but then I took a look at it and saw that it was going to have to be heavily edited because – duh – it's full of God stuff. God this, God that, God everywhere. Not only that but Judgement Day and marriage is like Christ to the Church and on and on. So I went on to the next. There's another old ceremony which a lot of people probably think is from the Book of Common Prayer that we use today, but it's actually from an earlier version, the prayerbook of Edward VI (who reigned in 1547–1553), and is apparently a different thing. It had a great sound, though, and everyone seems to know it – 'With thys ring I thee wed: Thys golde and siluer I thee geue: with my body I thee wurship: and withal my worldly Goodes I thee endowe.' And it said that as you say these words you move the ring along from finger to finger: 'with thys ring I thee wed,' you put the ring on the person's thumb. 'Thys golde and siluer I thee geue,' move it to the first finger. 'With my body I thee wurship,' the second finger, and so on. Looks like the pinkie doesn't get words said over it. You have to stop at the ring finger, which makes sense, but I had a vision of forgetting that and getting to the pinkie and saying, 'And this little piggy goes wee wee wee all the way home.' So *that's* out.

"This Edward VI ceremony also had some great stuff in it about fornication, which at nineteen was naturally of a whole lot of interest to me and would probably keep the guests awake, too. A little homily about how marriage was invented to stop rampant fornication. Well, they're hoping it will work for Lilla Vanilla, I thought. It went on about 'nor taken in hande unaduisedlye, lightelye, or wantonly, to satisfie mens carnal lustes and appetites, like brute beastes that haue no understanding: but reuerentely, discretely, aduisedly, soberly, and in the feare of God. Duely consideryng the causes for the whiche matrimonie was ordeined. One cause was the procreacion of children to be brought up in the feare and nurture of the Lord, and prayse of God. Secondly it was ordeined for a remedie agaynst sinne, and to auoide fornicacion. . .' Boy, there was something about how they spelled everything wrong that really lent weight to the matter.

"Then there was something called the Rose Ceremony, which is apparently some kind of famous alternative ceremony. And something called handfasting, which sounds obscene but is a pretty benign and hokey-sounding Druid thing.

"Well, as entertaining as all that was – and I was looking at everything at that point – it didn't quite suit, and that's when I stumbled on some lines by Emily Dickinson that got me thinking of my mother's marriage and how someday my father was going to be in that grave right next to her whether she wanted him there or not. And that seemed just the thing."

Ratchet glanced at Penpen just then and she was looking down at her lap and seemed sad. Ratchet wished she'd recite the actual poem, but Tilly just went rattling on.

"So there we finally were on the big day. Sure enough, Father's investments had kicked in, so that I had everything I wanted – the showers and parties, the engagement balls, the dinners and lunches and presents and rings. Cook made all the little petits fours and every tiny tricky thing I wanted, and I found the right music and even spent a couple of evenings with Burl, trying to get to know him. And there we were at last, going down the aisle between the rented chairs on our lawn. All was silent in our grove of trees as I spoke the verses I had so carefully chosen. Then I turned to Burl, who, unbeknownst to me, had been coached by the I Brake for Unicorns Committee. And he said, 'I promise that I'll listen to your dreams even if I can't always share in them. . .' and I think, uh-oh. 'I promise that I'll always respect the space you use to dream your dreams as long as you don't take up too much space.' And I think, what does *that* mean? Does he think I'm going to get *fat*? 'And that if you ask me to enter the room to share your dreams, please leave a window open because I get claustrophobic.' I can hear people nervously shifting in their chairs. 'And when you enter into my dreams please remember to walk gently because all our dreams are fragile. And when you leave please do not slam the door.'

"And he put the ring on my finger and tried to kiss me, but I was having none of *that*, not after those nincompoopy vows, and we went back down the aisle with the tiny muffled explosions of people's hilarity like thrown rice, and that was the end of that. At the bottom of the aisle, he went his way and I went mine. Of course, he tried to go my way for a while, but I kept kicking him away until he got the idea. I never bothered asking for an annulment or divorce because the whole business had satisfied my marriage needs and I never planned to do it again. The only thing I regretted was that now I didn't know what I'd do for entertainment, but Father solved that the following week, didn't he, Penpen?"

"He certainly did," said Penpen.

"What did he do?" Ratchet asked.

"He died."

THE BLUEBERRY BUSINESS

"Now," said Penpen, standing up to clear away plates. "Perhaps I should weed the garden before it gets too hot."

Ratchet helped her clear and then they went outside. Tilly lay in the hammock and Ratchet hung over the porch railing watching Penpen thin plants.

"He died," continued Penpen, "so then we had to decide what to do."

"And the first thing we did was to let go of all the servants," said Tilly.

"Release them is more like it."

"Undo their shackles is closer," said Tilly. "And they ran as fast as they could in any direction away from Glen Rosa. You could hear their little feet pitty-patting down the lane. Penpen and I were left alone in the woods with a very big house to take care of. The house was paid for, but we knew we'd have bills and we were uncertain whether the money we were left with would cover our expenses over the years. Penpen said we must think about that. I said I did all my best thinking at the tavern, so we got in the car and drove toward Dink, and that's when we found the remains of Edwards, the undergardener."

"Yes, so sad," said Penpen.

"And gruesome, too. Teenagers are really very self-centred. Oh dear, Ratchet, I didn't mean you. I should have said, more accurately, we were self-centred. It just never occurred to us that the servants would be eaten by bears on their way off the property. And they all disappeared before we had much of a chance to think about things, period. Anyhow, that's what happened to Edwards, the undergardener – bears. And we never found out what happened to the rest. We were particularly worried about Cook because she was such a juicy specimen, wasn't she, Penpen?"

"Plump. From all that cookie dough."

"And undoubtedly the bears had had their eye on her for some time. She used to give us little bites of cookie dough. Mother didn't mind."

"But after Mother died, Father put a stop to it," said Penpen. "He told us there was a child in town who had eaten cookie dough and the dough had gathered in a ball in the pit of his stomach and it blocked the entrance to his intestines, so that everything the child ate after that got bogged down until in a couple of weeks' time the child's stomach had grown until it looked like a watermelon and in another week it cracked open and the guts ran out in a river."

"We never believed him. That was the trouble with Father's

horrifying stories. He made them *too* horrifying. No one in their right mind would have believed them. We used to have to leave the room with our hands over our mouths to keep from exploding into laughter in front of him."

"He always thought we were muffling our tears. And was driven in remorse to leave chocolates on our pillows."

"So we were doubly determined not to let him see us laugh."

"It was the only time we got chocolates."

The words had been tumbling out of Penpen and Tilly like two tributaries into a river, and now they stopped and looked silently around the garden for a minute before Penpen continued.

"Anyhow, after finding Edwards, we drove into town and got the sheriff to bring him back to show him Edwards's remains. After I drove him through town he asked me if I had a driver's licence. Well, Tilly and I had never heard of such a thing. We thought this was pretty silly and were arguing with him about it when we pulled up in front of Edwards's remains and then he forgot all about the licence because the sight of Edwards's odd pieces seemed to put everything else right out of his head."

"For a sheriff he didn't seem to be real hardened to human detritus, did he, Penpen?"

"Well, he was new, remember? And he gaped and finally said, 'This is the work of a bear, all right.' And just then a bear came out of the woods and he drew his revolver and fired but missed. It scared the bear good, though, and it took off. 'God damn it!' he cried. 'That might have been *the* bear! The only way to find out is to shoot him dead, slit open his stomach, and see if we find any part of Edwards there!' and he kept shooting out the window into the woods in a most demented way. Tilly and I watched him quietly. Father had accustomed us to the vagaries of men.

" 'Well,' said Tilly, 'even if we hauled them all in for a line-up, it would be hard to identify which bear did it. They tend to look alike. You might have to take down an awful lot of bears to find the one . . . and I don't know where it will get you in the end. . .'

"So then the sheriff said, 'Miss Menuto and Miss Menuto. . .' "

"We just cracked up at that," said Tilly. She took up the thread of the story. "It sounded so funny. But he continued, 'Miss Menuto and Miss Menuto, do you mean to stay by yourselves alone on Glen Rosa, way out there in the woods?'

"We nodded because that was the plan, all right. And he said, 'Well then, let me give you a word of advice, get yourselves a couple of sturdy hunting rifles and learn how to use them.'

" 'But we already know how to shoot,' said Penpen because Father used to take us into the backyard for target practice.

" 'You also said you knew how to drive,' said the sheriff, but then he changed the subject quickly because he didn't want to appear to be offering us shooting lessons. The truth was that he found our company tiresome, very tiresome. 'I will give you the advice your daddy would give you if he were still alive. Now, I didn't have the pleasure of knowing him, never having had cause to come out this way, but I'm sure he would tell you that this is no place for two young ladies like yourselves to live. I've only just moved here myself, and to be honest I'm not sure it's a place for anyone but loggers and rough types. For one thing, it's too isolated. For another –' he searched around for another reason – 'it's full of bears!'

" 'Well, we *know* that,' I pointed out patiently.

59

" 'You've been pretty sheltered and your daddy isn't here to shelter you any more. Now, take this matter of the dead gardener. Man's body savagely ripped to pieces. Chawed on – ear here, part of a jaw there. This is no sight for two young ladies. It's bad dreams you'll be having tonight. And it's a shame to have this first traumatic sight of blood come so soon on the heels of your daddy's death. Two innocent young ladies like yourselves. Strangers to such gore.'

"Well, he was a nice man, but Penpen's and my mouths had been twitching ever since he began this speech.

" 'Actually, Sheriff,' I said, trying to get the words out without snorting, 'our mother . . . our mother. . .' and then I burst into loud guffaws. This set Penpen off. We had to stop the car and fall over sideways because we were laughing so hard.

" 'Here now, here now, give me that,' said the sheriff, shoving me over and taking the wheel. He stepped on the gas and drove away from the bear, shooting wildly out the window all the while. 'I've been to the lumber camps and off in places where there are no roads, but I've never seen bears the way you people have bears.'

" 'I suspect it's because of the blueberries,' I said, sitting up and wiping tears off my cheeks. 'We've got a powerful lot of blueberries.' And that set us off again and we started laughing fit to beat the band.

" 'This is none of it funny,' said the sheriff sternly. 'This is not a funny situation – this young gentleman being mauled by a bear.'

"And we thought that was hilarious, too. We pounded the seat in mirth. We always did laugh at the same things. And Penpen, through her hysterics, gulped and said as politely as she could, 'I'm sorry, it just sounded so funny because it's not just some young gentleman mauled by a bear. It's Edwards. The gardener. And he's been . . . *eaten*!' And then we both burst into hysterical laughter, which mid-snort turned into tears, and the sheriff, watching us sob, said, 'There now, that's better.'

"We sobbed the rest of the way to his office. We worried he had more fatherly advice that was going to make us giggle madly, but by then he was so completely sick of us he just said, 'Now, don't go driving this car no more without a licence, and I'll send someone out to take away the body . . . what's left of it.'

"And we couldn't help it, this put us in stitches, so we got out of that office fast, just calling, 'Don't worry. We won't!' and drove off, muffling our hysterics until we got a block away, where we began to laugh again and we laughed all the way home, taking turns to drive because we were laughing so hard that we kept hitting our heads on the dashboard.

"And that was the last time I let Penpen drive me anywhere because she kept smashing into bears all the way home. I don't know how she managed it. Most bears will get out of the way. And it's not like she *tried* to hit them."

"I have a knack for it," said Penpen modestly. "And after we got home I said to Tilly, 'Just imagine, Tilly, this was just like one of Father's horrifying stories.' 'But no chocolates on our pillows tonight, Penpen,' said Tilly."

They went inside and Penpen made sandwiches and lemonade. They took them to the porch, where they sat eating and swatting at bugs.

"I'd still like to know what happened to Cook and the rest of them," said Penpen.

"I bet Miss Greengage got somewhere unscathed," said Tilly.

"I don't know," said Penpen. "She took off at the rear of the property, and as far as I know, that path just goes deeper into the blueberry bogs."

"She said she knew a short cut."

"Well, she would have," said Penpen, turning to Ratchet.

"She was such a know-it-all," said Tilly. "She was one of those women who think their brains are being underutilized. Father used to say that her body was being underutilized because she was thirty and didn't have a beau and didn't seem to care about getting one. He said that's what made her so sour but also what made her such a good teacher, but she wasn't a good teacher. She was a terrible teacher. The only thing she really cared about was earning enough money tutoring to start up her own kennel and raise shelties. She had this big book about sheltie dogs which she kept in her room and brought down in the evenings to read in front of the fire. It was supposed to be her time and we were supposed to leave her alone and were usually more than happy to do so unless we were terribly bored and then we'd bug her. She was always saying, 'I can't wait for the day when I have enough saved so that I can buy my dogs and say goodbye to you little scumbags.' "

"She called you that?" Ratchet asked.

"Oh, we didn't mind, did we, Penpen?"

"Not at all," said Penpen.

"Miss Greengage tried every week to save what she could from her salary, but then she'd get a craving for good chocolate, expensive chocolate, and she'd drive all the way into Delta to the department store and blow her whole savings on a big box. Penpen and I would sit next to her by the fire as she looked at her sheltie book and ate her chocolates and we'd beg her to share, but she never would.

" 'Listen, you little scumbags,' she'd say, 'get your daddy to buy you your own chocolates.'

"And we'd say, 'But you know very well he won't.'

"Then Miss Greengage would always say the same thing: 'Then I guess money doesn't buy happiness. All that money and a dead mother and no chocolates. Seems a shame.' It was very cruel. We could never figure out why she was so mean."

"Now," said Penpen, "we realize she must have always been jealous of us. When you're a child you never figure a grown-up is going to be jealous of *you*. It's the grown-ups who seem to have everything. Children give adults far too much credit."

"Speak for yourself," said Tilly. "I gave Miss Greengage about as much credit as she gave me chocolate. After Father died, when we were searching for some way to pay our bills, I said to Penpen, 'Why don't we go into business like Miss Greengage always wanted to? Only something that doesn't require a lot of start-up funds because that was always her stumbling block.' Penpen said she had an idea for a business, and when I asked her what, instead of answering, she got all wide-eyed and cryptic like one of those obnoxious book characters and said, 'Why it's all around us!' This annoyed me so much that I hit her."

"I was afraid that with Father out of the way she was going to be one of those people who go around hitting people," said Penpen.

"And I was afraid that with Father out of the way she was going to be one of those people who are always making dramatic announcements and solving problems at the last minute because they harbour a lifelong dream of being the deus ex machina."

Ratchet didn't know what this was but didn't like to ask.

"It was our fear that with Father out of the way we would blossom into our true selves and we were rather afraid of what that might end up being," said Penpen.

"At least, I was afraid of what Penpen might end up being. I was pretty certain I was going to be all right, *myself*."

"You see, Father never let anyone's true self blossom. He didn't believe in it."

"At dinner he'd say a long grace which basically asked God to shape everyone's wayward souls in the way he, Father, thought best. Anyway," said Tilly, going on with the story, "Penpen said, 'Blueberries! Our business can be blueberries! The bogs are full of them. Let's can them and sell them.'

" 'You mean make jam?' I asked her.

" 'Not jam. Everyone in Maine makes blueberry jam. Let's make something distinctive and special. Let's make dessert sauce.'

" '*Dessert* sauce? What the hell is *dessert* sauce?'

" 'It's sauce you put on angel food cake, ice cream, pudding. Desserts.'

" 'Where did you ever hear of such a thing?'

" 'In point of fact, I made it up,' said Penpen proudly. 'But it has an interesting ring, doesn't it?'

" 'Well, if you made it up,' I said, 'where are we going to get a recipe?'

" 'We'll just make jam but more watery. It'll go further that way, too.'

"So that's what we did. At first we did it all ourselves. We made up our own recipe. We canned it. We sold it. One year we got bored and made jam as well, but that was the year the flies were so bad and were always landing in it and people who bought the jam were writing us angry letters about the number of flies in their jam and wanting their money back. Of course, we told them that anyone who was counting the flies in their jam had too much time on their hands. I was certain these people ate the jam, flies or no, so why should we give them back their money? Part of us wanted to sell nothing but fly jam after that, but we were tired of making the jam anyhow and weren't going to just to spite a few angry letter writers, although I suggested that we send all the angry letter writers a free jar of jam with a mouse in it."

"Anyhow, for years that's what kept food on the table, our blueberry business," said Penpen.

Tilly stood up on the porch and stretched and announced she was going to take her nap, and Penpen said she was going back to work in the garden. Ratchet went upstairs and lay on her bed, listening to the sea, staring out the octagonal window, and thinking of Tilly's stories.

They didn't eat until quite late because Penpen forgot about

65

making dinner until the sun began to set. Ratchet helped her peel carrots and chop things for soup, but they didn't talk much. It had been a long hot day, the kind of day so sultry and humid that the bees seem to sit in the air, suspended by its moisture.

Tilly came down to dinner and uncorked the Cointreau, which was still sitting on the table from breakfast.

"I wouldn't think that would go with vegetable soup," said Penpen.

"Cointreau goes with everything," said Tilly coldly and poured herself a second.

They ate dinner quietly, and the old grandfather clock in the hall bonged the late hour, before Penpen said, "Yes, that's what kept food on the table all those years, the blueberry business. During the canning season, life is a blur. There is time for nothing but the steady making of the sauce. You have to move fast, you can't even think, you just get into a motion over those blueberries and those pots, picking and boiling, ear cocked for the sound of the jam boiling over, dawn to sweaty dawn, dusk to aching dusk. And you have to know when to start canning. You can't do it when just some of the blueberries are ripe, things have to come together *just so*. There's a moment when everything is ripe. All at once. A critical mass!"

"Several times when we've had a bumper crop of blueberries, we've had to ask Myrtle in to help. But it's always a toss-up whether it's worth it or not. That woman can't see you put a jar down without deciding it should be moved a few inches over. A few inches over would be better. Thank goodness the raspberries get ripe first.

We pick them just to get our wrists in shape, just to get warmed to the motion, because in the canning season there is no time to think and plan, you have to move automatically, you have to can from some instinct within you, moving, moving. But years of late we've had to cut the production pretty drastically, haven't we, Penpen? We could have brought a crew in, but it's hard to find enough people. Everyone in these parts cans, and we all need help during the canning season," said Tilly.

They settled back in their chairs. Night had come thickly, darkly, like felt over the dining room windows through which pinpricks of starlight shone. Tilly burped.

"So did you ever find out what happened to Miss Greengage or the rest of them?" Ratchet asked.

"We found an arm in the bog once," said Penpen helpfully.

"When we were picking blueberries."

"Whose was it?"

"The very question we asked," said Tilly. "For all we know, it didn't belong to any of them."

"A stray arm."

"And yet you weren't afraid to spend all that time in the bog picking?" Ratchet asked.

"Oh, we were. We were scared spitless. We set up a system we use to this day. One of us picks while one of us watches with the rifle. We're both a good shot. It's worse for the one with the rifle, just standing in the sun, bees buzzing, worrying about being stung. And you can't shoot a bee."

"And not for lack of trying."

"Did you ever shoot a bear?" asked Ratchet.

"Never. I suspect they peeked out, saw the rifle, and headed elsewhere. You look at the size of a bear's head and you figure they've got to have *some* brains. We could have gotten twice the amount of berries if we both could have picked at once, but what profiteth it you to get twice the number of berries if you end up dead?" said Penpen.

"People called us the blueberry ladies," said Tilly faintly from where she was slumped in her chair.

"Until we made them quit. We hated that name. Then they just called us those queer Menuto women, which was quite all right."

"You didn't mind being called queer?" Ratchet asked.

"It was better than something cute like the blueberry ladies," said Tilly. "People could call us queer all they liked, we knew we weren't queer, didn't we, Penpen?"

"For the most part—" said Penpen.

The phone rang, cutting through the silence of the dark house like a sword and making them all spring out of their chairs at once.

HARPER

"You answer it, dear," said Tilly to Ratchet. "It's probably Henriette. I'm going to bed."

Ratchet was worriedly wondering what her mother could want at this hour and was thinking that it was very odd that she was calling yet again, so without thinking she picked up the phone and said, "Mom?"

"Mom?" said Myrtle Trout from the other end. "Now listen, you queer Tilly Menuto, I just called to say that when you are finished with the quilt piece you must phone me and I'll pick it up. I forgot to tell you that you're making the very last section. The very last, and we can't piece together the whole and start quilting until you're done."

"This is Ratchet."

"Oh, my heavens, you poor thing, can you put your aunt on?" said Myrtle Trout.

"Tilly," Ratchet said. Tilly was halfway up the stairs. "It's that woman who was here with the quilt piece."

"Myrtle Trout? What's that halfwit want?" asked Tilly, coming slowly back down. She put the receiver to her ear, leaned against the wall, and dizzily slid to a sitting position.

"I was just saying to your great-niece or whatever she is that your quilt piece is the last one and we're waiting for it, so if you could finish it soon, perhaps tonight, and phone when it's ready, I'll get in the Caddy and pick it up."

"In the Caddy? Did Burl buy you a great big car?" asked Tilly.

"Well, it eats gas something awful and it's terrible for parking and of course it was second-hand."

"I can see a car like that would be a powerful irritation," said Tilly. She was sitting sideways against the wall, and Ratchet was afraid she would slide right into a lying position any second. "We'll drive the piece in when we go into town."

"Now, Tilly, that's why I'm calling. I'll come and get it. I know you and Penpen. You'll just put that piece away and forget it and we won't see you for a month. Just call me when you finish and I'll come get it."

"We can't call out, Myrtle."

"Nonsense – oh, don't tell me you haven't had that phone line fixed yet."

"I'm done talking to you now," said Tilly and hung up. Her phone manners were sometimes a little rough.

Ratchet looked down at her. "Do you want help to your room?" she asked finally when Tilly didn't make any attempt to get up. "Penpen is in the kitchen washing up."

"Penpen should use the bathtub, it's easier to climb in and out of," said Tilly, taking Ratchet's hand to pull herself uncertainly to her feet.

"I mean she's washing the dishes," said Ratchet and put an arm around Tilly's waist so she could lean on her, and they negotiated the stairs one at a time.

"When Mother was alive she used to take us up to bed saying a line of poetry for every stair. I don't remember those old poems any more. But that's the kind of thing Mother did. She was a wonderful woman."

"Mmm," Ratchet said because she was straining to keep Tilly upright. Even her tiny weight was a lot to manage.

" 'Half a league, half a league, half a league onward.' I remember that one. But I don't remember most of them. The Dickinson one I said at my wedding was pretty good. I wish I remembered that," said Tilly. "It would have been nice if I could have said it to someone who wasn't such a dunderhead. I expect that if I had used it on someone better suited I would have remembered it. It's in one of the library books somewhere. My father bought a book of Emily Dickinson's poems for Mother for her birthday, but Mother thought it was hogwash. Not a Dickinson fan. After that, Father never bought her anything because he said he just didn't know what to get her, so he wasn't even going to try. What she wanted to *get* was out. But she couldn't. Because we were there, me and Penpen. She couldn't leave without us. But then she did, on a river of blood. Well, I suppose if I had used it on a better candidate, things would have been different. I wouldn't have sprinted down the aisle the way I did."

"And you'd probably have stayed married," Ratchet said, getting into a rhythm of drag, pull on the banister, lift Tilly a bit as she stepped up, drag, pull on the banister, lift Tilly a bit.

"But then what would have happened to old Penpen? I'm very fond of Penpen," said Tilly. Ratchet looked at her in alarm because she was falling asleep and they weren't near the bed yet. She gave her a gentle poke, enough to stir her until at last they were in front of her mattress and Ratchet could ease her down. Tilly immediately began to snore. It must be difficult being that old, Ratchet thought. How old was she? Eighty? Ninety? She turned. Penpen was standing in the doorway expressionless, a wet dishcloth thrown over her shoulder and her hands on her hips.

"Tomorrow I really should teach you to drive," she said and went back downstairs.

Ratchet went to her room and fell into a deep sleep until midnight, when she awoke to the memory of Myrtle Trout's face when she saw That Thing.

The next morning Ratchet milked the cow and Penpen showed her how to feed the chickens and gather the eggs. There were bits of hay on Ratchet's clothes and a faintly musty manury animal smell clinging to her. Back in Pensacola this would have signalled dirty and she would have needed to bathe, but here it just made her feel knit into the web of things and she didn't really want to wash it off. Nevertheless, she washed her hands before going into the dining room, where Penpen was dishing up breakfast.

"What is nicer on toast than poached eggs?" asked Tilly. "And what is that grace about happy the something and happy the something and blessed the sailors home from the sea?" began Tilly, when there was a knock on the door. Tilly stood up. "Damn that woman! I know what her problem is. Quilt piece, indeed. She just can't stand it that we have a house guest that she doesn't know every blessed thing about."

"You mean Myrtle?" said Penpen. She took a sip of coffee. She was really much too hungry to go answering doors, especially at this hour. Whoever it was could wait.

"Yes, Myrtle Trout," said Tilly. "She called last night demanding we finish the quilt piece immediately. She kept saying she'd drive in for it and I kept saying we'd go there because you know how I feel about protecting our privacy, Penpen. We can't have people showing up on the doorstep at all hours."

Penpen stood up looking alarmed. Poached eggs on toast had temporarily driven her new philosophy from her head. "Oh my!" she said. "Someone has *shown up*, Tilly. We must let them in! Even if it is Myrtle."

"Well, you're the blinking Buddhist, Penpen," said Tilly, sitting back down and beginning to eat her eggs again. "So I guess you'll have to deal with Myrtle. Only tell her not to make a habit of driving over. Tell her we'll do her idiotic quilt square tonight and drive it into town tomorrow morning. Pick, pick, pick."

Penpen left. Ratchet ate her eggs in silence. Finally Tilly looked up and said, "Myrtle presumes upon my good graces because she married Burl Junior, who is the son of my husband, Burl, and Thelma the wedding planner, whom he married illegally after he and I split up. After the wedding he went and lived in town. I would have given him a divorce if he had asked for one, but he never did. In the beginning it was because he hoped I would relent and be his wife now that we were married. Later it was on account of religion. He kept pouring out his woes to Thelma, who was still angry with me for not letting her plan my wedding, and the two of them cosied up with their common rancour, grudge to grudge, so to speak. They developed a flirtation based on my villainy. Then one day I guess Thelma decided that this hatred of me had gone about as far as it could go relationshipwise. She asked Burl to divorce me, but he wouldn't do it.

"Burl thought he was the laughing stock of the woods because of those vows of his, so he decided to show people he really wasn't a nutcake, and being not too bright, he figured the way to do this was to join the Catholic Church even if he had to go to Delta to find one. And once converted, he swallowed it all, hook, line, and sinker. He told Thelma that divorce was a mortal sin but he could probably see her Fridays. Well, you can imagine how that sat with Thelma. She charged into Delta and told the priest that he had to straighten Burl out. That Burl was committing a sort of polygamy in his heart if not exactly on paper. The priest was real sympathetic and told her he agreed with her and not to worry, he'd speak to Burl, only what he ended up telling Burl was that he had to ditch Thelma.

"Well, when Thelma found this out she was madder than a hornet in a jar and she went charging down to that silly little Catholic church and gave that priest an earful he didn't soon forget, although when she was done he just forgave her, so she gave up altogether, figuring there was nothing she was going to be able to do with that priest, he was just going to go on being stubbornly religious and she'd better concentrate on Burl.

"She went back and told Burl that if he didn't marry her, her daddy, big Ned Hassenfeffer up at the sawmill, who was known to be pretty able with a knife, would take care of him good.

" 'What do you mean, "good"?' asked Burl, because, let's face it, there were certain parts of himself he didn't want to go losing over some Catholic technicalities.

"Thelma made herself clear and Burl said, 'Well, all right, Thelma, but who will we find to marry us? Everyone knows I'm already married.'

" 'You just leave it to me, Burl,' said Thelma.

"Well, Thelma was a little slow, but she had long hours at the tavern slopping beer about to think things through, and finally one day she got in her car and went and got Burl and off they went.

" 'Where are we going?' asked Burl nervously because she was driving him right past Dink, Dairy, and Delta.

" 'We're going somewhere no one knows us and we're lying on the marriage licence.' Because after all those hours figuring things out, lying was still the best thing Thelma could come up with. 'And, by the way, you owe me a ring.'

"Well, Thelma got her ring 'long about their seventh wedding anniversary, as well as five children, two of whom died stillborn, which Burl kept insisting was a judgement. He drove Thelma crazy with his judgements. He got more and more involved with that Catholic church, but he would never take his family because their very existence, he said, was technically a sin. Anyhow, Burl Junior was one of those kids whose existence was clouded by the fact that he was a technical sin, and Myrtle never forgave me for that, although, really, none of it has anything to do with me. And the children wouldn't know they were technical sins if Thelma hadn't kept telling them, as soon as Burl's car pulled out of the driveway bound for church Sunday mornings, that that's what their father considered them. 'There you sit,' she would say, 'technical sin one, two, three. I'm surprised we even bothered with names. We could have just given you numbers.' And Thelma brought it up whenever she saw me, which was about once a year – a mite too often as far as I was concerned – but you know how it is, some people are like that, always running over and interrupting your peace. Course, you know Penpen's philosophy. . ."

Just as Tilly said this, Penpen came in. Next to her was a girl a little bigger than Ratchet. She had long, straight, slightly ratted hair of odd lengths as if it had been cut with a razor, and she dragged a suitcase next to her.

"This is Harper," said Penpen.

When Penpen opened the door she was so startled she couldn't speak. There stood a very pregnant woman and next to her a girl around Ratchet's age. The girl was holding a suitcase and looked inquisitively inside the house as though she couldn't bear the suspense any longer but must go in and see it. The pregnant woman showed no such curiosity. She just looked hard and determined.

"This here's Harper," said the pregnant woman.

"Oh!" said Penpen because she couldn't think of anything else to say. For a moment they stood mutely in the sunshine. Finally she recovered and said, "I'm Penelope Menuto."

"Yeah," said the woman as if this were superfluous information, and then she opened up her battered patent leather pocketbook, fished through it until she found a squashed pack of cigarettes, shook one out, and began to smoke it. Penpen was as startled by the appearance of the cigarette as she was by the two of them on her doorstep. Clearly today was going to be a day of surprising appearances. No one had ever just shown up on Glen Rosa's doorstep. It was such a long, hard road that if anyone did mistakenly turn off the main road and start heading toward them, they figured out their mistake long before they hit the last dirt track. Most turned around by the first bear.

The woman lit the cigarette and took a long draw, and the girl, as if she could contain herself no longer, pushed gently past Penpen and stood in the vestibule gaping toward the parlour.

"It's awful quiet here," said the woman finally, letting out a stream of smoke. "I thought it would be noisier."

"You thought it would be noisier?" said Penpen.

"You know, with kids and all," said the woman. "To be honest, I thought it would be a perfect hell, but this is nice. You can hear yourself think. What do you do – keep them all locked up?" And she gave Penpen a playful little punch on the arm that offended Penpen very much. She didn't think this woman was crazy: there was too much determined anger in her eyes. But she didn't think she had very good manners either.

"Now listen," said Penpen, "I think there's been some mistake."

"What do you mean? They told me back where I come from — and let me tell you, it's been no picnic getting all the way out here today — they told me you'd take *anyone*. That that's the thing about you. You wouldn't refuse a big girl like Harper."

"Oh," said Penpen. She thought to herself that she had only started espousing this Buddhist philosophy last week and here already Ratchet and this other girl had shown up at her door. Perhaps Tilly was right; perhaps it was fortunate they didn't live somewhere more accessible. At this rate they'd shortly be out of bedrooms. She wondered who the *they* were that this woman was referring to and how they knew about Penpen's Buddhist philosophy. But I suppose, she thought to herself, that it becomes part of the collective unconscious, when you make a decision like this. Or is that Jungian? The problem was that she began espousing these philosophies before she understood their complete ramifications. She had better be cautious. She had better do more reading before she espoused anything else.

"Well, that's true," she said finally. "Where did you say you came from again, dear?"

"Helox. It's down south and west of here. Like I say, it's been a long drive."

"Did you want to come in, too?" asked Penpen, keeping one eye on Harper, who was wandering around the parlour, picking up knick-nacks and putting them down again.

"Me? No, I wouldn't be caught dead in a place like this. No offence."

"None taken," said Penpen automatically. Her mind was on

Harper, who was wandering now from room to room, peeking around corners as if looking for something. "And you say everyone is saying that I will take anyone in?"

"Well, I don't suppose they mean you personally," said the woman, stamping out her cigarette on the nice white porch and shaking another out of her pack.

"No, of course not," said Penpen, looking at the cigarette butt distractedly. Apparently, the collective unconscious had included Tilly in the scheme of things. "I don't suppose there's anyone specifically who told you so? A name I might know? Someone from Dink or Dairy?"

"What would I be doing talking to someone from Dink or Dairy when I live in Helox? Course, now I'm getting out. I don't live in Helox no more as of yesterday. I'm getting out with the baby –" she patted her stomach – "and heading up to Canada. It was a French Canadian who got me this way."

"Oh," said Penpen and tried to look sympathetic, but she was having a hard time following what was going on here aside from the fact that apparently she was to take this woman's teenage daughter in while she went to Canada. "You're going to look for the father, you mean?"

"Him? Oh no, I got no use for him. It's his mother I'm looking for. I figured she's my best bet. She seemed like a real nice woman from all the stories he told me, and I thought, you know, maybe I'd bed down there while I have her grandchild. Those French Canadians – family's real important to them, you know? And I got none of my own. Not since Harper's mom took off."

"Oh, so you're not Harper's mother?"

"Well, duh. If I were Harper's mother, what would I be doing leaving her here?"

This one stumped Penpen.

The woman took a puff of her cigarette and went on. "Anyhow, that's what I'm saying, Harper's mom split. Course, she took off when Harper was only pretty much of a baby herself, so I've been stuck raising her, not that I minded, you know, but you know what it's like raising a kid. It's a big responsibility. And I was only fifteen when I got left with her."

"I never had any children of my own," said Penpen.

"Well, yeah, but you know, you got 'em around. You know what they're like."

Penpen nodded, thinking that they'd only had Ratchet a few days. How did this woman know this stuff? It was uncanny. You just open the door to the unconscious and look what happens. Perhaps she would take up meditation and a macrobiotic diet, too. It was all happening so fast, this change from no real philosophy to Buddhism. And she really knew *nothing* about it.

"So anyhow, Harper and I've already said our goodbyes and I guess I'll go now," said the woman.

"So trusting," Penpen thought aloud.

"Huh?" said the woman.

"I just think it's so trusting for you to leave Harper with complete strangers like this."

"Well, like I said, you've got a reputation. Although, if you don't mind me saying so, it's a hell of a remote spot and what've you got all the bears for? Is it kind of like a security system? To keep them from escaping?"

"To keep who from escaping?" asked Penpen.

"The orphans," said the woman.

And then Penpen got it. "Oh, my heavens!" she said and sat down with a thud on the porch steps. She reached up, grabbed the woman's forearm, and pulled her down beside her. "I think we'd better start all over from the beginning."

"And so," Penpen said to Tilly and Ratchet after Harper had gone upstairs to unpack and she was finishing telling them all this, "that's when I realized that the woman, Miss Madison, had meant to take Harper to St Cyr's. She drove all the way from Helox because someone had told her that at St Cyr's orphanage they'd take anyone, even such an old girl as Harper."

"How could she have made that mistake?" asked Tilly.

"Well, it's a big house, lot of property. I suppose we do look like an orphanage, Tilly."

"No, I mean the turn-off. The turn-off to St Cyr's is at least another ten miles up the road."

"Yes, but people forget about our road because no one ever uses it. They just say take the first turn-off from Dink."

"But I don't understand. She *isn't* an orphan, is she?" Ratchet asked.

"Well, Miss Madison doesn't know. Her sister, Harper's mother, took off years ago, and from what Miss Madison told me, she may well have come to a bad end, but at any rate she never came back for Harper."

"Harper's father?" asked Tilly.

"On death row for killing a chimpanzee."

"Can you get the death penalty for killing animals?" Ratchet asked.

"And the zookeeper," added Penpen. "And there might have been a few more odd bodies."

They were all silent for a moment. Then Penpen heaved a sigh and went on, "Apparently, Miss Madison didn't really want to be saddled with Harper, but she did the best she could although she could never warm to her, as she put it, and now with a baby of her own on the way, she realizes she flat out doesn't want Harper and also that she just can't manage two kids."

"But Harper isn't a child," said Tilly. "She's Ratchet's age. She could baby-sit the new baby."

"It's what Miss Madison thinks she needs to do right now. Anyhow, odd or not, it's not as strange as it was before I found out she mistook us for the orphanage." Penpen was thinking thank God she had cleared that up and didn't need to go on a macrobiotic diet after all. Although it was a shame to let go of the notion that Miss Madison had found her way there via the collective unconscious. Still, just because that hadn't happened *this* time didn't mean it might not happen another time. She must buy guest towels.

"So why didn't you just redirect her to St Cyr's?" asked Tilly.

"Two reasons: first of all, whatever shows up on your doorstep—"

"I know, you have to take it in," said Tilly, rolling her eyes.

"And second, because, to be honest, I wasn't entirely sure Harper would make it there. Miss Madison seemed determined to be rid of her before she 'went all softhearted again'. And when I told her we weren't the orphanage, that she had taken the wrong turn-off, I didn't hear her say, Oh, I'd better go back and get new directions. She just kept saying HUH in a disturbingly vague way, and I had visions of her letting Harper off on the road and telling her to hitch-hike the rest of the way. She seems bound and determined to get to Canada tonight."

"She's going to drive all night in her condition?"

"She's a very determined woman."

"Goodness," said Tilly.

What Penpen didn't say was that she also thought, here was company for Ratchet. So far they seemed to be keeping Ratchet entertained, but she didn't think she should do nothing but milk the cow. She should have someone to play with. Did girls still play at thirteen? She tried to remember what she did at thirteen, but the teen years ran together in her head right up until the grand tour. She always had her nose in a book, and, of course, she had Tilly for companionship. She was hoping maybe Harper was heaven-sent. Penpen believed in things being heaven-sent. She thought you need only keep an eye out for them. Penpen spent the whole day looking for clues that Harper was heaven-sent, but she found precious few of them.

When Harper finally came downstairs, which she did after inspecting all the upstairs bedrooms without any regard for anyone's privacy, Tilly said, "Why don't you put on a swimsuit, Harper, and we'll go down to the beach?"

"I don't own a swimsuit," said Harper.

"We'll have to get you one in town," said Penpen.

"They're going to think there's a sudden run on young ladies' bathing attire," said Tilly. "They're going to start ordering in swimsuits for thirteen-year-old girls by the dozen."

"I'm fourteen," said Harper. "Why don't you just order me one over the Internet? I'll surf until I find one I like. I just need your credit card number. Have you got any gum?"

"No," said Tilly, who hated gum. She thought it was repulsive. "And I don't know what you mean about surfing either."

"I mean on your computer," said Harper.

"We don't have a computer," said Penpen. "Do you mean you can shop for clothes on the computer?"

"Yeah. We didn't have a computer either, but imagine not knowing you can shop there. Huh. Well, if you don't have any gum, what about some cigarettes?"

Penpen burst into laughter. She couldn't help it: Harper had taken on the look of a young desperado. But on their way down to the beach, Tilly leaned in to Penpen and said, "Chewing gum and cigarettes. I hope you know what you're doing, Penpen. I think we're going to have trouble with that girl."

"Well, you can hardly blame her for wanting to smoke," said Penpen. "Her mother, or rather her aunt, but the only mother she's known, has just dropped her in the middle of the Maine woods with a bunch of complete strangers. What's she supposed to want to do? And that Miss Madison clearly smokes like a chimney when she's nervous even though she looks about ready to drop that baby any minute."

"You should have brought Miss Madison in and given her breakfast. I would like to have had a look at her," said Tilly.

"Too late now," said Penpen as they laid their towels on rocks. "She's probably halfway to Quebec."

"OK now, Ratchet, ready?" said Tilly, wading out. Ratchet trailed behind wearing a T-shirt, shorts, and one of Tilly's cardigans over her swimsuit. It took her a few minutes to get everything off. It took her longer than necessary because all the way down the cliff and into the water she wondered if Tilly and Penpen had actually seen That Thing. Obviously, Myrtle Trout had, but there had been no reaction from Tilly and Penpen other than being appalled that Myrtle had ruined her sweater. And the incident was never mentioned again. If they hadn't seen it, what would they say when they saw it today? In the back of her mind, like a tiny minuscule guarded thread of hope, was the thought that maybe her mother had been wrong and people wouldn't mind so much, that it wasn't quite as grotesque as Henriette thought. That Penpen and Tilly *had* seen it and simply not thought much about it after that. If that was the case, she didn't mind taking off her things. On the other hand, suppose they were going to see it now for the first time. In that case, she would rather not take anything off. She would just rather not swim. Every time she thought of this she stopped unbuttoning.

Tilly, who was waist-deep in water, turned around and said, "Come *on*, Ratchet."

Harper was sitting up on the rocky slope that went down to the beach, sucking on the end of a long blade of grass and looking discontented. "It's hot here in the sun. Isn't there any shade around? Nobody told me there was going to be any ocean here. If you ask me, this isn't much of an orphanage. There's nothing to do. No water slides, no make-up classes, no sewing club."

Penpen realized with alarm that they had forgotten to tell Harper that this wasn't St Cyr's. Harper was wandering around the parlour when Penpen had her talk with Miss Madison. And Harper hadn't even come out to say goodbye to Miss Madison. Miss Madison had said they'd already said their goodbyes. Penpen was still surprised not to see a few tears, a little clinging, a little begging not to be left, but this was not Harper's way. And because Penpen had spoken at length with Miss Madison, and, when she finally did go back inside, it was only in time to help Harper save a vase from being knocked off a table, she had completely forgotten to fill Harper in.

"Oh dear, oh dear," said Penpen.

"Don't sweat it," said Harper generously. "I figured Maddy was lying to me. I didn't think orphanages had things like water slides. She's a lunatic, that Maddy." Harper opened the picnic basket and dug in.

"Is that what you call your aunt, dear?"

"Well, I called her Mom until I was five, and then she said to cut it out and call her Maddy. That when I called her Mom it made people think she was older than she was and it scared off men. Maddy likes men, all right – oh my frigging God, what's that thing on her shoulder blade?" said Harper, standing up and pointing at Ratchet as her T-shirt came reluctantly off.

"Shhh! Hush! Shhh! Hush!" said Penpen agitatedly.

86

Ratchet immediately squatted under the water.

"It's disgusting!" said Harper. "Is that why no one has adopted you?"

"Oh dear," said Penpen.

"Of all the rude little twits," said Tilly, wading back to Ratchet, who remained squatting with her arms wrapped protectively around herself. "Come, Ratchet. What a mouth on that girl. And what does she mean, why no one will adopt her? She isn't *up* for adoption. What a bizarre notion."

"Well then, what's the deal? What's she doing here? Her parents leave her here because of that thing?" asked Harper, still staring down through the water at Ratchet, waiting for her to get up so she could get another glimpse of it.

Penpen and Tilly suspected that this might be getting a little too close to the truth, so Penpen pulled Harper by the arm toward the path. It wasn't in her nature to peoplehandle anyone, but she saw no other way of removing Harper, whose attention was so completely riveted to Ratchet's shoulder blade.

Ratchet blinked away tears, mostly from the pressure of being the centre of so much unwanted attention. Tilly could see this, so she left her alone and began swimming back and forth, taking her morning horizontal constitutional as if nothing had happened, while Penpen dragged Harper up the path to the house to explain to her where she really was. When they had finally left, Ratchet didn't know what to do, so she put her clothes on and sat on the ocean floor where it was shallower and let the waves splash over her hot face, holding her breath when a big one crested. She sat like that a long time until Tilly said, "Well, I guess I'll get out now."

Ratchet nodded and pulled herself out of the water. It wasn't that she was going to give up learning to swim, but she wasn't going to tackle it any more that day. Whether Tilly understood this or not, she didn't mention it again, and they went up to the house to change. The only thing Tilly said, she said when they were on the white stone path, almost to the house; then she blurted it out as if speaking to the trees, the forest, Maine, as if voicing to the universe a long-stifled complaint: "The world is full of fools!"

Meanwhile Penpen was having a useful and elucidating conversation with Harper, who was sitting on the Victorian red velvet love seat in the parlour, her knees and ankles together, looking very nervous.

"It is a shame," Penpen began, "that your aunt didn't see fit to keep you with her."

"It's all right, I'm used to it," said Harper. "What is that thing on that kid's back anyhow?"

"Her name is Ratchet, dear," said Penpen. "Now, I'm sure this has been a perfectly miserable day for you."

"Well, it hasn't been a great one," admitted Harper. "I didn't really think she could do it, you know, leave me. I thought she'd turn around. Maybe she still will. She cried on the way here, you know." Harper had eaten everything in the picnic basket except the bag of sunflower seeds. Those she had carried up from the beach. As she chatted to Penpen and realized this interview was going to be a cinch, she opened the bag and began sucking on them, spitting them out afterward into the potted-palm planter.

"That's rather a messy thing to do," began Penpen mildly,

looking at her lovely potted palm. "That's actually a completely disgusting thing to do. Why are you doing that?"

"You can't swallow them," said Harper. "That is, I suppose some people do, but Maddy told me that people who swallow seeds get things growing in their stomachs. Of course, I didn't believe her, but still, I can see you don't want to swallow them. Some people have little pouchy pockets in their intestines. You or I might easily have those without knowing. You wouldn't want a seed getting stuck in one. I don't even chew them. I just like to suck the salt off them."

"Um-hmm," said Penpen, resuming polite tones, but when Harper spit another mouthful into the dirt of the planter, Penpen lost it and yelled, "DON'T DO THAT!" It startled Penpen, who couldn't remember the last time she had raised her voice.

"Hey, don't yell at the orphans," said Harper imperturbably, putting another handful in her mouth.

"I wasn't yelling. I never yell," said Penpen, who still could not believe she had done so. "Let's go outside and start again. You can spit in the garden all you like." They walked to the side garden, where Harper became fascinated with the sundial. "I've heard about these. I wanted one for my garden. Does it really work?" she asked Penpen, putting her hand gently on the arrow.

"Yes, of course, as long as the sun is out."

"And no moving parts. It's a wonder, this thing," said Harper.

This startled Penpen. "Of course, the earth's the moving part. Yes, it's a very nice sundial, isn't it? My father got it in Italy. When we were on the grand tour."

"The grand what?"

"Tour. Tilly and I spent about a year travelling around Europe when we were teenagers."

"Hey, I wouldn't mind going to Europe. Don't suppose Maddy and I will ever have the money, though."

"We're kind of getting off track here," muttered Penpen. "Please sit."

"So you never told me what that thing is on that kid's shoulder blade," said Harper.

"Harper, the reason I wanted to talk to you is because I think you're under a misapprehension."

"A what?"

"This isn't an orphanage. We're not St Cyr's. This is Glen Rosa."

This stopped Harper in her tracks and she looked Penpen over as though perhaps Miss Madison had left her someplace where she would be cut up and sold for dog food. Noncomestible meats, that would be sooo like Maddy, Harper thought. "What is Glen Rosa?" she asked coldly.

"This is our house. It belongs to me and Tilly, and Ratchet is our young relative, come to spend the summer."

"Oh, she is, is she?" Harper rattled on unthinkingly, words spilling out of her as she tried to come to grips with this. "Come to spend the summer with her aunties? Isn't that precious. Only I suppose at the end of it she'll be going home. Well, what am I doing here and what will I be doing at the end of the summer?"

Because Penpen had been rather focused on keeping her Buddhist philosophy and finding a companion for Ratchet, she hadn't thought this through. This was the first time it occurred to her that the summer *would* come to an end and Ratchet *would* be going home and what in the world, indeed, would they do with this girl? "I don't know," she said and sat down suddenly in the hammock, which was suspended over a bed of phlox, disturbing a bee, which stung her, causing her to cry out and run into the house for ice. As she ran cold water over the sting she thought about the matter. The Buddhists never said what to do with what had showed up on your doorstep if you took it in and it proved less than charming. When she got back, Harper was lying in the hammock. She had picked the heads off all the phlox. Well, fair enough, thought Penpen and went inside to make some more lunch.

Penpen set lunch on the table just as Tilly and Ratchet came in. They changed and Penpen asked Harper, who seemed to have a boundless capacity for food, to join them. It was a strange, silent lunch. Tilly was annoyed with Harper, whom she found rude and insensitive. Penpen felt terribly guilty because she didn't know what to do with Harper or what to tell her was to be done with her. Ratchet was uncomfortable because she thought everyone was thinking about That Thing and was upset that it was just as grotesque as Henriette had always claimed. And Harper knew that no one at that table was terribly glad to see her, and it made her want to be even ruder than she had been, but she had no opportunity because no one was speaking to anyone else. They were all lost in their own private little emotional storms, and when the phone rang they jumped.

It's Maddy changing her mind again, thought Harper.

It's that evil Myrtle Trout, thought Tilly.

It's St Cyr's coming to the rescue, thought Penpen, who was

perhaps the most far gone, driven closer to the edge by guilt.

It's Mother, Ratchet thought.

Penpen picked up the phone and was so discombobulated when she heard Henriette's voice, because she so wanted it to be St Cyr's, that she handed the receiver wordlessly to Ratchet.

"Well, *really*," said Henriette after Ratchet said hello. "They are getting seniler and seniler, aren't they? Doesn't she even say hello any more?"

"I don't know," Ratchet said quietly, hoping it would cause Henriette to lower her voice, but when she looked toward the dining room table, no one was paying any attention anyway. They were all drumming their fingers.

"I've called to tell you not to call here even if you get the notion to because I never seem to be in these days. In fact, I may not be here at all for a couple of weeks."

"Oh," said Ratchet. There was a pause while she digested this. "Where are you going? Are you going away?"

"Yes and no. I am going. But not away precisely. Where am I going? Well, where *am* I going? I'm probably staying with a girlfriend for a few days."

This sounded very fishy. In the first place, Ratchet's mother had no friends. "What girlfriend?" Ratchet asked.

"You don't know her!" she snapped. "You don't have to know every friend I make. The point is, don't worry if I don't answer the phone. In fact, don't even bother calling."

"I can't call out anyhow. Tilly and Penpen's phone doesn't work that way."

"Oh my God, haven't those old bats ever fixed their phone?"

"No," said Ratchet.

"Are you keeping That Thing covered?"

"Yes," Ratchet lied.

"Good," said Henriette and hung up.

"Anyone want any dessert?" asked Penpen when Ratchet returned to the table.

No one answered, but Penpen went in and got the pudding anyway and they all pushed raisins around the rice for a few minutes. Then Penpen said, "What did she want?"

"Oh!" Ratchet almost swallowed a raisin the wrong way. "She called to say that I shouldn't bother calling her because she wasn't going to be home."

"Did you tell her you can't phone out anyway?" asked Tilly.

"Yes. She said she's going to stay with a girlfriend," Ratchet continued.

Penpen and Tilly nodded.

"But she doesn't *have* girlfriends!"

Penpen and Tilly looked at her inquiringly.

"She didn't send me here this summer because she has cancer, did she? She isn't going into a hospital, is she?" Ratchet pleaded, searching their faces for signs of subterfuge.

"Oh, my poor child," said Tilly, "is that what you thought? Good Lord. Of course we would tell you if she had cancer. As far as we know, your mother is in the pink of health. If she says she's going to stay at a girlfriend's, then she probably is."

"But why would she do that when she has a perfectly good

apartment of her own?" Ratchet persisted, sounding tortured.

"Maybe it had to be fumigated," said Tilly.

"Or painted," said Penpen.

"Then why wouldn't she tell me *that*?"

Harper, who had greedily finished her rice pudding and was grabbing Penpen's untouched bowl from in front of her, said, with rice grains spilling down her chin, "Girlfriend my foot! Your mother has a boyfriend."

And they all stopped eating and stared at Harper as they realized that, of course, she was right.

DR. RICHARDSON'S LONG ARM

As well as spitting sunflower seeds into the planter and eating her own portion and everyone else's at mealtimes, if she could get away with it, Harper brought the Menutos news of the outside world. She followed them around individually and en masse for days, explaining everything you could do on the Internet. Their thoughts were on the notion of Henriette's having a boyfriend. Who could he be? They thought it certainly put a new light on Ratchet's summer visit. But they listened with one ear while Harper explained how you could get newspapers, catalogues, all kinds of information from a computer.

"It doesn't seem possible that all that stuff is available for free," Tilly said once, but Harper just shushed her, although gently, and went on because Harper knew all about the Internet and the information was practically spilling out of her. She had spent many hours in after-school care surfing the Net, but Maddy had never had any interest in what she had learned.

Ratchet had used school computers, too, but didn't know nearly as much as Harper because she didn't have access to one for hours after school the way Harper did. Henriette had never bought a computer, and she always made Ratchet come home right after school because she didn't want to pay for after-school programmes and didn't like the idea of her making friends.

Tilly and Penpen, of course, didn't even own a radio, much less a television or computer. If Maine were invaded by aliens, said Harper, they'd all be the last to know.

"I'd want to be the last to know," said Tilly. "What possible advantage would there be in being first?"

In the busiest of their blueberry-canning years, Penpen and Tilly explained to Harper and Ratchet, they had had more contact with the outside world because as the business grew, they needed the help of Mr Feebles, who brought them cartons and canning jars and drove away with the packed product, marketing and selling it for them for a commission. He often wanted to talk about what was going on in the world because that was what Mr Feebles did. If he had had better opportunities, Penpen said, he would have been a political scientist. Life had forced him into the salesman trade, but he discussed the world situation with anyone who would listen. Tilly and Penpen drove him wild. "How can you have no opinion on anything?" he would ask them indignantly. "I can forgive an intelligent person having the *wrong* opinion, but how can you have *no* opinion?"

"How can we have opinions if we have no idea what you're talking about?" asked Penpen gently.

"You gals ought to keep abreast of things," said Mr Feebles.

"Why?" asked Tilly grumpily. "What good does it do you? It seems to me, from what you've been telling us, that everyone these days knows everything about everyone and the split second it happens, too. What do they do with all this information? What does it get them? It just clutters up their peaceful quiet time. It seems to me, from what you've been describing, nobody *has* peaceful quiet time any more. Television, bah! Radio, bah! Newspapers, magazines, bah, bah! Sounds like the world is running off half-cocked, people getting zapped with their little hits of information. Needing it every day. Zap, zap, zap. Well, deliver me. Contagious. Like hoof-and-mouth disease. I hope you're not contaminated. Don't go trekking it all over our property."

"Very funny," said Mr Feebles. "You're a queer couple of ladies, is what you are."

"Yes, yes," said Tilly, "those queer Menuto women. I know all about it. Now, you drive gently on those rutted roads and don't go breaking those blueberry jars."

"Like I would. Did I tell you ladies about the plan this new First Lady has?" asked Mr Feebles. He tried to explain to them again how the present government wanted to change the medical system, but Tilly said that she didn't plan to get sick anyhow.

"But," said Penpen to Ratchet and Harper as they all sat on the porch and she remembered this and reminisced a bit and they all kept passing Harper things to eat in hopes she'd stop talking about the Internet for a few minutes. Penpen and Tilly had become accustomed to Ratchet, who was so quiet she was like having a little ghost around the property. Harper's chatty presence was an entirely different thing to get used to. "Do have another fig, Harper. As I was saying, but after that Tilly did get sick and she always blamed it on Mr Feebles and his putting ideas in her head. She got so sick that I finally had to get a doctor, so I drove the Daimler into town, leaving Tilly reluctantly behind. The doctor who came out was Dr Richardson, who had an arm three inches longer than the other because of an accident in the woods. Someone else's, not his.

"One day Dr Richardson got a call to come quickly to a logging site. A logger had accidentally hanged himself when he fell from a branch and his jacket got caught about his throat. He had somehow gotten himself into such a precarious position that the only way to reach him was from the branch beneath him and no one was tall enough to do that. There was a chopper on the way, but it didn't look like it was apt to get there before the ultimate damage was done, so they had sent for Dr Richardson with the idea of having him on hand to verify the cause of death.

"Dr Richardson raced out, and when he got there, the logger was still miraculously alive. Dr Richardson was probably the tallest man in the woods. He was six foot seven and looked like Abraham Lincoln, and he could see that they couldn't quite get up to the man to save him. No one could figure out how the poor logger had gotten up to the branch he was on. They were all standing around on the ground speculating about it when Dr Richardson got there. Meanwhile, the poor man's face was turning blue.

" 'Help me climb up,' Dr Richardson barked, starting up the tree.

" 'Ain't nothing you can do, Doc,' said a logger watching from the ground. 'He's a goner.'

" 'Nonsense,' said Dr Richardson. 'I'll declare the goners around here. You just help me get up that tree.'

"So they helped him up. They wanted to lend him some cleats, but no one had feet as big as his and anyway there was no time. The hanging logger was gasping his last.

" 'What are you going to do? You got something in your black bag to treat this type of thing?' asked a logger as they watched Dr Richardson's feet disappear into the branches.

" 'No, you goddamn idiot,' said Dr Richardson. 'I'm going to try to reach up high enough to lift him from underneath to loosen the jacket around his neck until the helicopter can get here. I think I'm just' – pant, pant: he was panting and calling down to them as he climbed – 'tall enough to reach the soles of his shoes and boost him from beneath.' But he wasn't. He was a good three inches too short. But that didn't stop Dr Richardson. He put his left hand against the tree trunk and reached with his right arm. He just kept reaching until his straining arm almost came right out of the socket and his palm made contact with the soles of the man's shoes. Then he lifted the man enough to get some slack in the jacket around his neck. He stood like that, precariously balanced for an hour until the helicopter came and dropped someone down on a line to rescue both the logger and Dr Richardson. The logger walked away with nothing worse than a sore neck, but when Dr Richardson got out of the hospital (he tore a ligament in his shoulder without even feeling it), he discovered his right arm was three inches longer than his left. And if you ask him about it he just snorts and says, 'Something in my black bag! Goddamn idiots!' That's the type of man Dr Richardson is," Penpen finished.

Tilly rolled her eyes.

The phone rang. Ratchet got up to answer it, wondering who it could be, since her mother had said she wouldn't call for a while.

"Sweetie, how are you?" purred Henriette.

Henriette had never called Ratchet "sweetie" before, and it crossed Ratchet's mind that she might be ill, after all.

"I'm fine," said Ratchet warily.

"I had to call. I was talking to Hutch, actually Hutch was making me dinner and I was telling him what it's like to be a mother, and he said that naturally I must miss you."

"Who is—" began Ratchet, but Henriette was intent on doing both parts of the conversation.

"Well, of course you're having a wonderful time. Canoeing and swimming and fireside chats about the great authors. Aunt Penpen is such a fan of the great authors, isn't she?"

"Canoeing?" said Ratchet, but Henriette interrupted again.

"Summers in Maine. It sounds just like a novel, doesn't it? 'Whose woods these are I think I know. His house is in the village though.' What flowers does Penpen have growing? Tell her from me that she must grow hollyhocks! If I had her garden I would plant hollyhocks all around the house. Oh goodness, Hutch is putting things on the table. Must run." And Henriette hung up.

Ratchet stood holding the phone receiver.

"How is your mother?" asked Penpen when Ratchet had returned to the table.

"You realize all you said was 'Who is' and 'Canoeing?' " said Harper.

I also said, "I'm fine," thought Ratchet.

"Oh, and also 'I'm fine,' " said Harper, screwing up her face as her brain backtracked through the conversation and at the same time going through all the nuts on the table in a steady workmanlike way.

"Where did Tilly go?" asked Ratchet. Tilly often left the room when Penpen went on and on about the type of man Dr Richardson was. She had escaped to her room to lie down, so Penpen, deciding Ratchet needed a change of subject and also because Tilly wasn't around to censor her, continued to tell them about meeting Dr Richardson for the first time.

She said it was unusual for a town the size of Dink to have a doctor in residence, but Dr Richardson was paid by the lumber companies and the mill to be on hand. He treated the loggers for all kinds of complaints from foot fungus to loneliness. He knew everything about the woods and its inhabitants. In a feudal way, she said, he was a kind of king of the woods, overseeing the workings of it all. He looked much younger than his years, keeping spry by leaping over huge fallen cedars and climbing up trees to extract what was left of loggers pinned under boughs. The kinds of accidents loggers had in the woods required a doctor with great agility and a strong stomach. Dr Richardson had both. The first time they met him was when Tilly got sick and Penpen drove frantically into town. He was having coffee with his wife, but he left it and got in the Daimler next to her. He drove with her for half a mile before he demanded she stop and switch places with him.

"Are you in a state of overwrought nerves or do you always drive like this?" he asked her.

"Both," she answered honestly. "No one ever taught me or Tilly how exactly. I haven't had much practice because Tilly is much the better driver, so she always takes the wheel."

They were silent most of the way to the house although Dr Richardson did say once, "What's with all the bears?"

"We think it's because of the blueberries," said Penpen.

"Oh, you're the *blueberry* ladies," said Dr Richardson, eyeing her with new interest.

"We really hate that name," said Penpen. "We're also called those queer Menuto women. If you must call us something, we prefer that. People don't understand our living alone so far out in the woods."

"I like the woods," said Dr Richardson. "I have colleagues in Boston who don't understand why I practise way the hell out here. They think *that's* queer."

Penpen liked him a good deal after that and even better after he had treated Tilly.

Dr Richardson stayed in Tilly's bedroom an efficient amount of time. Long enough to diagnose and treat her but not so long that Tilly felt he was in any danger of deciding to move in with them. And he was sympathetic enough to make her feel well cared for but not so much that it got sloppy and silly and annoying.

He came down the stairs finally, bag in hand, to where Penpen was nervously pacing.

"Well, she's had a heart attack," he said.

"Oh, dear God," said Penpen.

"Not really surprising at her age," he said.

"Well, you'll pardon me if it's surprising to *me*," said Penpen. "It's not what I expected. You don't expect anyone you know to have a heart attack. Except, perhaps, Mr Feebles."

"Him? Hmmm. He's a young man still."

"He's a fat man," said Penpen. "And sometimes when he discusses social assistance, he goes very red in the face."

"He's not eighty years old, though. Still, point taken," said Dr Richardson. "It's a shock, I'm sure. Have a drink."

"No thanks," said Penpen. "That's much more Tilly's thing."

"No, well, all right. I'll have one, if you don't mind."

Penpen went over to the liquor cabinet, fumbled with the key, and poured him a sherry. He looked at it and said, "So this is your idea of a drink. Huh!" and tossed it back in one shot.

"Another?" asked Penpen.

"No thanks. I have to drive," he said meaningly.

"Oh dear, and I do hate leaving Tilly."

"No problem," said Dr Richardson. "I'll call my wife and have her pick me up."

"Our phone doesn't work that way," said Penpen. "You can't dial out."

"Never heard of such a thing," said Dr Richardson.

"It's true. Oh dear. I'm sure it seemed a good idea to Father back then. He wasn't anticipating Tilly having any heart attacks when he did it. Of course, she was only twelve years old at the time." And Penpen's eyes welled up as she realized that Tilly was no longer a young girl, as if seeing her white kinked hair and wrinkles and suddenly realizing what they meant. That old age had come and what had seemed like an interesting diversion – the first few grey hairs, the stooping body – wasn't just a pleasant novelty. They weren't going back; they weren't ever going back. Their youth, their *youth*, was gone. It was as if, unwitnessed, out here, safe in the woods, they should have been out of time as well. If no one had seen their passing, they shouldn't have passed. She wondered if Tilly, lying upstairs alone, was suddenly as aware of it as she was. "I guess I'll have to take you back. There's really nothing else to be done. Well, let's go right away. I don't want to get back too late. I don't want to leave Tilly there with this dreadful news all alone in the dark."

"If it happens again, give her an aspirin right away, understand?"

"For the pain?"

"No, no, it dissolves clots."

"*Clots?*"

"Just remember to give her one, all right?"

"Well, how do I know she has had one? I didn't know this time."

"Give her one if you have the slightest suspicion. It won't hurt her. The thing is, you're quite right. She may have silent heart attacks. She may have had some already and she may have more. Or she may have not-so-silent ones that she won't tell you about. Just do your best."

Dr Richardson drove the two of them back to his house, and then Penpen turned around and drove home, feeling very alone.

But she supposed she would feel this way even if she and Tilly lived in the centre of a bouncing family. Driving home to disaster always made you feel alone.

Tilly had several more heart attacks over the next few years. Penpen always gave her aspirin and paced around and then went for the doctor, who learned to follow behind in his own car. The more heart attacks Tilly had, the tireder she became, but neither Penpen nor Dr Richardson was silly enough to suggest she go into a hospital. Penpen was grateful to Dr Richardson for this and one day awoke to realize she was carrying a torch for him. She had been almost pleased that Tilly had had the last heart attack because it brought him out again for the first time in two years. The force of her feelings for a man twenty years younger than herself, and at her age, upset and rather pleased her.

"Don't you think it's a little odd that I'm not having heart attacks, too?" she asked Dr Richardson as she gave him his sherry and he studied it with his usual scorn for all drinks not whisky.

"Why should you?" he asked, packing up his bag to leave again until the next crisis.

"Tilly and I have always been so close. We're twins, you know. We've always done everything together."

"I would never have guessed you as twins. Not identical, obviously."

"No, no. We're chalk and cheese, Tilly and I."

"Well, there you have it, then."

"But we have plans to die together," said Penpen, and then much to her embarrassment a tear slid down her cheek as she thought how very much closer Tilly seemed to dying than she. "I mean, she seems to be in much worse health than me. Ageing faster." She had secretly always thought she looked much younger than Tilly. Then another tear slipped down her cheek at the thought of Tilly's approaching demise. She wiped it off as she wondered if Dr Richardson had noted how much younger she looked than Tilly.

"Well, you never know," said Dr Richardson, "you could get a stroke suddenly or a massive coronary, and boom, it's all over for you in one fell swoop, as opposed to Tilly's gentle decline. I've seen people push on for years after these attacks. The problem is that the heart muscle is slowly destroyed, so that it has to work harder. Watch her for oedema."

"Oedema?" said Penpen, but her mind wasn't on oedema; it was riveted by the thought of a massive heart attack and going suddenly – out like a light. Such a thing had never occurred to her. All this frank talk of her sudden catastrophic demise had taken all the fun out of her mild flirtation. She slumped.

"Water retention. Means the heart isn't doing a good job pumping. Whole system is going to the dogs."

"I'll watch for that," said Penpen faintly and showed him to the door.

Ratchet thought it was odd that Penpen had just told them all this about Dr Richardson because later that same afternoon, when Tilly got up from her nap, his name came up again. There was a knock on the door. Tilly went to answer it and there standing on the doorstep was a stranger. Tilly hadn't seen Miss Madison before and thought that she was on her way to Canada, if not already there, so she thought that suddenly everyone was taking the wrong turn-off from Dink. She was very pleased that it was not Penpen who had opened the door. They'd soon be out of spare bedrooms.

"You've come the wrong way! Go back! Go back!" she said to the surprised Miss Madison, who had perhaps had too many surprises already in her short life to startle easily and said, "I've come for Harper."

"Oh," said Tilly, "you're Harper's, er, guardian."

"Yeah, that's me. So if you'll tell her to get her things together. . ."

Tilly nodded and put Miss Madison on the hall bench and went in search of Harper. Penpen found Miss Madison there and said, "Oh, my goodness. You've come back."

"Yes, for Harper."

"Oh, that's much the best thing, I think. Were you driving along and realized you'd missed her? It's not so easy giving up a child, is it?"

"Yeah, it is," said Miss Madison, wiping her nose. She had a cold. "But, anyhow, I didn't drive nowhere. What happens is, I'm coming through the woods after leaving Harper here and a bear runs right smack into the front of the car and takes out a headlight. Scared the wits out of me, if you want to know the truth. So I go into town and find a garage, and while I'm getting the thing fixed I start to have contractions, so I'm like all bent over, and the garage man's wife calls the doctor in town."

"Dr Richardson," said Penpen.

"Yeah, that's him."

"Lovely man."

"Whatever. And he finds me and examines me back at his place and says that I've got blood pressure, so I have to lie down half of every day. No driving. Otherwise, he says, the baby could be premature and also I might have it on the road up to Canada. So I'm staying at this guest house in town."

"In Dink?"

"Yeah."

"Can't imagine whose that would be."

"Yeah. And I think, well, as long as I have to stick around I might as well get Harper back."

"Ah."

"I don't have hardly any money for the guest house either."

Penpen thought, Another one. "Would you like to stay here?" she asked. "You have, after all, turned up on our doorstep."

"No thanks," said Miss Madison. "Nothing personal, but this place gives me the creeps."

Harper and Tilly came in. Harper was carrying her suitcase and looking relieved.

"Well, anyhow, thanks for having her. Harper, you got anything to say?" asked Miss Madison, getting up and putting one hand on her stomach.

"Why do I have to say anything?" asked Harper. "It was never my idea to come here."

"Say something, Harper!"

"It's been a slice," said Harper, picking up her suitcase.

The two of them walked down the steps not speaking to each other. "As if," said Penpen to Tilly as they discussed it at dinner, "as if Harper didn't even require an explanation. As if an explanation was unnecessary."

"In a way, I suppose it would be," said Tilly, chewing on her second piece of chicken. Having Harper leave had given her a great appetite. "After all, if Harper's mother or aunt or whatever she is decides to keep her, what choice does Harper have? But she ought to have had a choice. I'm not saying I wanted her as a permanent house guest, but, I repeat, she ought to have had the choice. It's not right dumping her all over the place."

"Well, perhaps dumping her here was just one of those impulsive mistakes people make. Maybe that's the last time she'll dump her. Maybe it was just a blip on that woman's radar screen, that's all. We all make bad decisions now and then. And she's pregnant. Pregnant women are supposed to be crazy."

"I don't go around making bad decisions. And it's still not right," said Tilly stoutly and went to the liquor cabinet for the crème de menthe. "I worry that woman is going to dump her again, only this time on the road to Quebec. I shall lie in bed all night and toss and turn over it. It's extremely aggravating."

"I'm worried, too," said Penpen, standing up to fuss with the dirty dishes. "But I don't see what we can do."

However, neither Tilly nor Penpen need have worried because two days later Harper returned. Ratchet was looking out her bedroom window when a car drove into the yard. It was an old beat-up four-door and the woman Ratchet guessed to be Miss

Madison emerged looking very pregnant and a little crazed. Her shoulder-length hair lay in tangles around her face and she was muttering, "Bears, bears, bears." She slammed open the trunk and waited for Harper to heave her suitcase out; then she returned to the car, slammed the door, and drove away. Harper stood in the yard looking at the house. Ratchet knew that Tilly was taking a nap and Penpen had her beekeeping outfit on and was attending to her hives. Ratchet thought beekeeping looked fascinating and had been thinking about going out to watch Penpen and ask her about it, but she didn't want to be a bother. She wondered when Harper would come into the house, but Harper just continued to stand in the yard looking uncertain. Ratchet heaved a sigh and went downstairs and on to the porch. Although Ratchet was quiet she had gotten used to receiving more attention than she ever had before since coming to Glen Rosa and she was aware that Harper, who was so much more high-maintenance, tended to eclipse her. It made Ratchet feel vaguely peevish.

Harper didn't know Ratchet was there and was wiping her nose on the back of her hand. Ratchet stood and watched, trying to figure out what to say, until Harper, looking up, suddenly noticed her and said, "Jesus Christ! Don't spy on a person like that."

"Tilly's taking a nap and Penpen's in the garden with the bees."

"Huh," said Harper. "Some homecoming." She dragged her suitcase across the yard and up the steps and sat down on a chair. "I'm famished. I haven't had lunch. And we drove all the way from Dairy."

"What were you doing in Dairy?" Ratchet asked.

"Getting a second opinion. Maddy heard that there was another doctor in Dairy. She got tired of lying in bed. Also she said it's getting awfully expensive just lying around that boarding house. She said the woman is gouging her – fifteen bucks a day for a room and two meals and not even her own bathroom and she says she doesn't want to see Maddy's waters breaking all over her wood floors."

Ratchet didn't have any idea what Harper meant by waters breaking. It sounded dangerous to her.

"Anyhow, Maddy keeps telling me like she always does how much she loves me. How she could hardly stand to let me go like that. She even cried, right? Well, I wasn't surprised. I knew she'd made a big mistake. Big mistake, I thought to myself when she drove off that first time."

Ratchet didn't say anything, but she wondered what had happened between the time Maddy told Harper she loved her and the return to Glen Rosa. Harper looked at her and, as if guessing her thoughts, said, "All because I wanted a swimsuit. She took me with her to Dairy because she didn't want to drive the roads alone because Dr Richardson said it was dangerous for her. So we drive in and I'm asking her if I can please have a swimsuit. When I was little and Maddy still had her job at the factory, I had swim classes. Then she lost her job and had to find pickup work all the time and I couldn't have swim classes any more. There was a swim team at school that was free, but I needed a swimsuit. I'd ask and ask and ask for one, but Maddy said it was a luxury. Like some twenty-dollar swimsuit is a diamond ring or something. So then I tried to make money baby-sitting, but these people I sat for said their kids didn't like me – the rotten little nose-pickers – and I didn't get any jobs after that. So anyhow, we're driving to Dairy and Maddy is high because she's so excited at the idea that this different doctor is going to give her a different opinion about her blood pressure and I tell her that if I had had that swimsuit I wanted I could have been swimming with you guys and who lives in Maine and doesn't even own a swimsuit and she's so happy she says maybe we'll go swimsuit shopping to celebrate after she sees this new doctor because she can use the money that she would have had to piss away on the boarding house and maybe she'll get herself some post-baby stuff, too, because she's sick to death of these second-hand maternity dresses she's wearing and then she drops me off with a buck and tells me to get an ice cream at Woolworth's and I'm in there eating fries when she storms in and sits in the booth and says it's time to go and I say, What about my swimsuit, and she says, Swimsuit, swimsuit, don't I ever think of anything else? She's sick of hearing me asking for stuff all the time. In fact, she's just sick of me, period. And then she won't talk the rest of the way back even though I keep saying, You've still got the blood pressure, don't you? And she finally says, Yeah, and look, it's just not working out. She can't afford to get all worked up like this, like I'm the one who got her so worked up, and that for the health of the baby maybe I'd better spend some time here while she figures out what to do, and she's all so preoccupied that bears are skidding right by the front wheels of the car and she's not even batting an eyelash. Pregnant women are bonkers. I'm never getting pregnant."

Then Harper went inside, up to the room she had stayed in before, and put her suitcase on the bed with a bang. She came down wearing cut-offs and a T-shirt and said, "I'm going swimming in this. Want to come?"

Ratchet shook her head and picked up a book. She was thinking that if she gave Harper her swimsuit and she was the one who swam in T-shirt and cut-offs, they'd both be happy. But it didn't seem very grateful somehow to Penpen and Tilly, who had bought it for her.

After dinner, as Harper finished relating the whole story again to Penpen and Tilly, who didn't seem in the least surprised to see her, Penpen said, "Well, of course the doctor in Dairy said the same thing! Dr Richardson is a very *good* doctor."

Tilly rolled her eyes and changed the subject by rapidly emptying two glasses of crème de menthe and then saying to Ratchet, "And what did *you* do all afternoon?"

"I read a book I found in the library called *Vanity Fair*," Ratchet began.

Penpen interrupted, "Oh, I loved that book. Let's see, I read that one three times, or was it—"

When Harper interrupted *her*: "Well, you wouldn't catch me reading some book three times. What's the point? You already know how it ends, dontcha?"

"Penpen has read everything in Father's considerable library three times," said Tilly.

"And sometimes four," said Penpen. "And sometimes five. I read all the books and then I started back on the 'A's – Father arranged the library alphabetically and we still keep it that way. The second time through went much quicker because when you know what's coming, you don't read quite so thoroughly. Your eyes tend to skim."

"Why don't you go to the public library and get some new books?" asked Harper. "Dairy has a public library. We passed it on the way to the doctor's." When she saw Penpen's and Tilly's blank looks she said, "Jeez Louise, it's the Internet all over again, isn't it?" She carefully explained the concept of a public library to them. When she was done, Penpen said, "Oh, I couldn't do that. Take all those books out for free. It seems like cheating."

"Sounds to me like you just don't know how to have fun," said Harper and crankily grabbed the last piece of raspberry crumble.

"I suppose we could drive into Dairy once a month for books, couldn't we, Tilly?" said Penpen uncertainly.

"It's a very long way to go. Especially in the winter. Our turn-off is quite impassable a great deal of the time. We have to get supplies when we can," said Tilly.

"We could still go in the summer. And the fall."

"Do what you like, Penpen."

"Yes, but you know you always drive, Tilly."

"Speaking of driving, Penpen, when are you going to teach the girls to drive?" asked Tilly. "You keep saying Ratchet should know how, but now that Harper's back, both girls should really learn. Why don't you start tomorrow?"

"Oh dear, yes," said Penpen, pouring herself some more tea and spilling it on the tablecloth.

"Too cool," said Harper.

Ratchet didn't say anything. She really didn't want to learn to drive. Actually, she didn't mind learning but she didn't want to be responsible for driving others around. Suppose she got them stuck in a ditch and a bear got them?

They went to bed after that. All night long Ratchet had dreams about bears and doctors and babies being born wearing little swimsuits and driving little cars.

THE GARDENING HAT

The next morning Ratchet awoke even earlier than usual. She was getting used to waking up at sunrise to milk the cow and separate the cream. At first she had found it difficult, but now she was falling asleep earlier at night, full of sea air and exercise. She had come to welcome this time alone in the morning. One of the things she wasn't used to was having people around all the time. It had always been just herself and her mother or more often just herself. Now there was always someone around and always people to eat with. It was exhausting. Even if she never said a word, she had to keep up with the flow of conversations and activities. But in the morning all was still. She was alone in the stillness of the universe a little while before all the confusion began. It was as if she could hear it ticking, check in on the life at the very centre of it, its wellspring that everyone somehow knows, before it was covered by noise.

This morning Ratchet awoke even before sunrise and Penpen's

old rooster started crowing. She sat on the edge of her bed in the dark. Her bedside clock said four-thirty and she knew sunrise would be in about half an hour. She was thinking that today was the day Penpen said she would teach them to drive and she was not at all happy at this prospect. She didn't want to be at the wheel of the car and didn't want to be in the car when Harper drove it. Ratchet couldn't imagine that anyone would want to be in a car when Harper drove it.

By the time Ratchet had gone out in the rosy orange light of early morning, milked the cow, cleaned up the barn, and separated the cream, her stomach was in such knots that she could not eat the oatmeal that Tilly had made, which was perhaps a good thing. Tilly was stricken with conscience because although she knew Ratchet liked getting up early and milking the cow, she felt she was sloughing off one of her duties. Shortly after Harper arrived the first time, Tilly had decided to make up for it by being the one to make breakfast every day. The problem was she didn't really know how to cook and she didn't have a very discriminating palate. The oatmeal might be mostly gluey water or it might be, as it was today, a thick mortarlike substance studded with mouldy raspberries that had made it past Tilly's failing eyesight. But Tilly felt it was such a virtuous thing for her to be paying attention enough to make breakfast regularly, as opposed to when she happened to remember, that it never occurred to her that they might be breakfasts nobody wanted to eat.

"I can't eat these raspberries, they're mouldy," Harper said loudly, picking them off and putting them on the tablecloth.

"Please use a saucer," said Penpen. "You'll stain dear Mother's tablecloth."

"I thought dear Mother stained her own tablecloth," said Harper sourly, because Tilly had told her part of the story.

"Not this one," said Penpen.

Ratchet breathed a sigh of relief and began to pick off her own mouldy ones. She had been worrying quite a bit that they might make her sick. She didn't think they would kill her unless she was allergic to penicillin, which as far as she knew she was not, but she didn't like the idea of them whizzing around her system, and although in the end she had suffered no ill effects, she was glad she no longer had to shovel them down. This was the good thing about Harper. She did things which at first seemed unbelievably rude and obnoxious but which you secretly wished you could do yourself. Her remarks were less offensive once they realized that she was simply determined to speak the truth and be done with it. There didn't seem to be any hidden corners in Harper's soul, and she wasn't interested in allowing other people theirs. Often, as in the case of the raspberries, this alleviated delicate problems.

"Well," said Penpen, eating a pile of pancakes. Tilly had made raspberry pancakes, too. It was much harder to see if any mouldy ones had been put into these, and Harper and Ratchet were staying away from them. "Are we going to learn to drive today?"

"You bet," said Harper, going into the kitchen to help herself to more oatmeal.

"Good," said Penpen. "I will teach you."

"How come Tilly isn't teaching us?" asked Harper. "Isn't she the one who can drive the best?"

"Tilly is going to work on the quilt square. Besides, I have more patience for this type of thing. I can sit in a calm Zen-like state in the passenger seat. Calm is very important for a driver, beginner or no," said Penpen, folding her napkin in her lap and assuming a Buddha-like expression.

Ratchet looked down at her lap. "I don't think I really do want to learn." It was very hard to say.

"Why not? You don't have to take off your sweater for it," said Harper through a mouthful of oatmeal.

Spoons clattered to the table, and Tilly gave Harper a long look of exasperation. Harper was so intent on getting two pieces of bread and honey into her mouth at once that she didn't notice until she looked up to grab the honey jar again. "What? That's why she won't learn to swim, right? Because she doesn't want to take off her sweater. So I'm just pointing out she can't use that as an excuse. You don't have to wear a swimsuit to learn to drive."

"Honestly, Harper," said Tilly, getting up and clearing the table.

"WHAT?" said Harper again.

"You could try to be a little more . . . subtle," said Penpen finally.

Ratchet didn't know where to look. Her cheeks burned.

"Anyhow, if she doesn't want to learn, she doesn't want to learn. I'm ready," said Harper, getting up.

"Why don't you go help Tilly with the dishes, Harper, dear," said Penpen. "Come, Ratchet, I'll show you the Daimler."

Ratchet had already seen the Daimler, but Penpen took her outside and made her acquainted with the driver's seat and all the little buttons and levers. "You see, there really isn't anything to worry about. It's all straightforward and this is an ideal place to practise. No one uses the road. And we don't even have to go on the road yet. We can just drive in circles, round and round the yard."

Ratchet thought of bears on the road and having to get out to switch drivers. She knew that once they were on the road they would have to take the car a long way before there was a place to turn around. She looked at the yard. How long could they drive in circles there before they all got hopelessly dizzy?

"I'll sit in the front passenger seat where I can put my foot on the brake if I need to," said Penpen. This was even less reassuring because Penpen was fat and arthritic and Ratchet doubted very much she could stop the car in time if she needed to.

"Ratchet," said Penpen quietly, "it may be dangerous to learn to drive. I give you it probably is a dangerous thing, learning to drive. But you have to understand that with Tilly having heart attacks, and we really have to anticipate more of them, and the two of us being twins and having decided to die together, it's important that you and Harper can get yourselves out of here if you need to. I need to teach you while I *can* teach you. It's the only way I can with good conscience keep you here."

Ratchet nodded and was surprised at the twinge of unease she felt when Penpen said, "can with good conscience keep you here". Until that second, if you had asked her, she would have said she just wanted to go home.

"Well, are we ready?" cried Harper, coming out to the front porch and spitting sunflower seeds all over the yard.

"She's like a lit firecracker," said Penpen as Harper approached them. "You find yourself mesmerized, waiting for it to go off."

"It's exciting in a way," said Ratchet.

"What's exciting?" said Harper, jumping into the back seat and spitting the rest of the seeds through the window.

"We're saying there's an air of waiting for something to happen around you," said Penpen tactfully.

"Like expectations," Ratchet fumbled.

"Don't have any expectations," said Harper. "Expectations will screw you up. I never have them. So don't go around telling me I inspire them or anything. Jesus."

"Well!" said Penpen cheerily, getting out her driving manual. "Since Harper's the more enthusiastic driver, why don't you come in the driver's seat, Harper, and Ratchet, you go in the back. This is the book that Tilly and I sent for when we were told we had to get a licence. Of course, it was all too complicated and we decided just to skip it, and a lot of it didn't seem applicable to our situation anyhow. But since you are learning I thought we may as well try to do it right this time and, who knows, maybe I'll learn a thing or two, too. Let's see, let's see, OK, let's start here," said Penpen, rapidly flipping through its pages. "Stop signs. What to do at stop signs. Well, that certainly seems clear enough. Of course, we have no stop signs around here. Even at the turn-off there is none, but, gracious, you'll know whether to stop or not. You stop when you don't want to get squished like a bug on the windshield, that's when you stop. Any idiot could figure that out. Wait, here we go – four-way stops. Now, this may be useful. I believe they have one of those in Dairy. OK, it says that the person to the right has the right of way. That seems clear enough. Unless all four cars are there at once and then everyone has someone to their right. What do you do then? They don't tell you. That's just the type of problem we ran into the first time we read this book, I believe. It's all too ambiguous. And listen to this, if a motorcycle and a car are both driving at fifty miles an hour (well, already you can see it will never apply to us. We never go over twenty. NEVER) and they must brake suddenly, who will stop sooner? Well, my goodness. Who cares? I think we can skip that part, too. It disguises itself as motor vehicle knowledge, but really it's physics, which any other time would be fascinating but not right now, not while you're trying to learn to drive. Let's see, is there anything useful in here? No, I don't believe there is."

Penpen threw the manual out the window in disgust and sat with her arms folded over her chest. "Don't tell Tilly I did that. She said this manual would be no good. I hate it when she's right and I hate it even more when she finds out she was right."

The girls promised not to say a word to Tilly.

"OK now," said Penpen, "first you put on your driving gloves."

"Maddy doesn't wear driving gloves," said Harper.

"A lady always wears driving gloves," said Penpen.

"Well, that explains why Maddy doesn't have any," said Harper and guffawed.

"Well, perhaps the driving gloves are optional. Let us move on. Now, here is the clutch and here is the brake and that big pedal is the accelerator. It makes the car go."

"Vroom, vroom," said Harper.

"What is that, dear?" asked Penpen.

"I said, Vroom, vroom," said Harper.

"I heard what you said. I just don't know what it means," said Penpen.

"It's the sound that sports cars make," said Harper. "Jesus, welcome to the twentieth century. How do you turn this thing on? Oh, wait, I know. This key turns, right? And you step on the gas. I've seen Maddy do it a thousand times."

Harper turned the key and stepped on the gas, and then before Penpen could say anything, she stepped on the gas again. The car shot forward. Unfortunately, it was parked facing the cliff edge. Not only did Penpen not lean over to use the brake, she covered both eyes with her hands and screamed. Ratchet in the back seat, watching the cliff edge race toward them, opened her mouth but nothing came out. It felt as if all the air were rushing into it. Harper made some kind of sound that was surprise and annoyance and terror and suddenly moved her foot, luckily finding the brake and not the clutch and flooring it. The car slammed to a complete halt five feet from the drop to the sea. Ratchet opened her door, rolled out, and lay hyperventilating in the grass. Harper had the sense to turn off the ignition and sat panting in the front seat blinking back tears, and Penpen had a heart attack. Her first.

At the time it was not at all funny. Later, they always referred to it as the time Harper almost scared Penpen to death.

"My arm," said Penpen, clutching her left arm. "Oh, my left arm. Oh my God." She was pale and sweating and clutching her chest. Harper turned to her and through her shakiness yelled out the window, "Ratchet! Penpen is, I think, hey, this old granny is having a heart attack. I think she's having a heart attack. I think she's having a heart attack." She kept trying to get a handle on the situation and inspire others to action, but that was all she could think of to say.

Ratchet remembered the story of Tilly's heart attacks and ran inside for the aspirin, and Tilly came out at a run carrying the bottle. They opened the collar of Penpen's blouse and gave her an aspirin to swallow, and then Tilly said, "Move over, Harper, either get out or get in the back. I'm driving Penpen to the doctor."

"Maybe you should just bring him here, Tilly," said Penpen. "I don't feel like I could survive the trip in. I really don't. I feel very queer."

Tilly looked as if she was going to burst into tears, but she said, "Yes, of course, you're right. Old fool. Old fool. Girls, get Penpen into the house and put her on the couch. I'm going for the doctor."

Harper and Ratchet were able to hold Penpen upright long enough to get to the couch. Tilly sped away at a great pace – well over twenty miles an hour. "Oh, please don't speed, Tilly," said Penpen faintly at the sound of the car starting up. "Girls, go after her and call out not to speed. I don't want her having an accident on the way there."

"Don't you worry about her," Ratchet said. "You have to lie quiet."

"I'll go yell at the old bat," said Harper and ran outside screaming, "SLOW DOWN!" Tilly was long gone, but she thought it would make Penpen feel better to hear her calling it as if Tilly were still in earshot, so she called again, "SLOW DOWN! THAT'S RIGHT! NO NEED TO RUSH!"

"That's better, thank you, dear," said Penpen. She was lying on the couch in a cool sweat. Ratchet didn't know what to do, so she got her a pillow and a blanket from upstairs and a glass of water.

"Don't give her water!" said Harper. "You're not supposed to give accident victims water. They can lose consciousness and upchuck it and choke on their own vomit."

"Oh!" said Ratchet worriedly and ran back to pour the water down the sink as if it were a dangerous substance. She felt as if she should be doing many things quickly but had no idea what else to do, so she paced back and forth by the couch until Penpen opened her eyes and said, "Don't worry so, dear. I've seen Tilly through several heart attacks and she's just fine."

"She ain't exactly bright-eyed and bushy-tailed," said Harper. "It didn't exactly improve her none."

"But she's still alive and ticking," said Penpen, and that's when, much to Ratchet's amazement, Harper burst into tears. She sat right down and, with no apparent embarrassment, sobbed gently into her indrawn knees. There were tears flowing down her legs and her nose ran. She didn't make any attempt to get a Kleenex, thought Ratchet, she just let it all wash over her. Penpen said, "There, there." It looked as if Penpen wanted to pat Harper. Her hand reached out, couldn't quite make the foot-long journey, and fell limply to the floor. This scared Ratchet even more.

It was three hours before Tilly arrived with Dr Richardson. He transferred Penpen to the bed upstairs and then took Harper aside.

"Listen," he said, "it was not, I repeat, *not* your fault that she had a heart attack. She is ninety-one years old. It was going to happen any moment. At the worst, the very worst, the episode in the car brought it on an hour or so earlier than it would have happened naturally."

"Yeah, OK," said Harper, looking at the wall.

"She had it because she was meant to have it," said Dr Richardson, trying again to meet Harper's eyes and finally giving up because Harper wouldn't.

"She is just keeping up with me," said Tilly. "Of course, she's still several heart attacks behind."

"Don't go giving her ideas," said Dr Richardson, closing his bag and getting his coat. He had driven his own car behind Tilly's. They walked him out to it.

"I knew Penpen shouldn't have taught them to drive, but she likes teaching things and I don't. Zen-like calm, indeed."

"Well, life's a dangerous business," said Dr Richardson vaguely.

After Dr Richardson had driven away, Tilly went upstairs to comfort Penpen.

"He's a *very* good doctor, Penpen," said Tilly.

"He's a dish," said Penpen faintly and fell asleep.

The next few days Penpen stayed in her room. Harper and Ratchet took meals up to her when Tilly remembered to make them. Ratchet was too shy to announce that they had once again skipped lunch, and for the first two days after Penpen's heart attack, Harper was too demoralized to bring it up, but on the third they all began to recover their equanimity, and when it was three o'clock and no lunch, Harper strode out to where Tilly was tending Penpen's bees and said, "What do you have to do to get a meal around here anyway?"

Tilly looked at her blankly through her beekeeping veil, but Harper couldn't see Tilly's expression and decided that Tilly was merely aghast. Harper was used to people being aghast at her. "I'm hungry," she said. "And so is Ratchet."

"Ratchet knows she can make herself lunch whenever she likes," said Tilly.

"Yes, but she wouldn't. Not that mouse," said Harper. "She'd starve to death first. And nobody told me. I don't know how you grannies feel about these things. And I don't want to be put out on that road with those bears."

"Nobody's putting you out on the road," said Tilly mildly, going back to her bees. She was very worried about Penpen and unfazed by Harper's histrionics. "I'll be up to get lunch soon."

"By then it will be dinner," muttered Harper. "It's not as if I haven't been getting my own lunch for the last umpteen years. It's not as if I were asking you to do that."

"Would you like to prepare lunch for us all, then?" asked Tilly.

"I don't know," said Harper sulkily, walking back inside. She didn't know what other people would think of her cooking. She hoped that if she muttered all the way back inside, Tilly would not be able to tell if she had said yes or no.

"Of course, when I was growing up, we always had Cook. It would not have occurred to me that young ladies could get their own lunch. Or Penpen either," Tilly went on, not aware that Harper had already gone up to the house. "But if you already know how to make lunch and have nothing you would prefer to be doing. . . The problem is that I simply must get to these bees and it is so time-consuming. I don't know how Penpen does it, really. Not at her age. It's no wonder she had a heart attack." And then Tilly had a little weep, but there was no one around to see, not that they could have seen through the veil anyway, and when she turned around again, Harper was gone.

"That girl's attention span is too short," she said to herself and then forgot all about Harper and lunch and didn't appear back at the house until six-thirty, when she realized she was late making dinner. Good thing they had a late lunch, she said to herself.

When Harper got up to the house, Ratchet was just going out with a book. "Well, aren't you hungry? Aren't you ever hungry?" she asked.

"Yes," Ratchet said guardedly.

"Because that old bat down there ain't making lunch."

Ratchet didn't say anything. She could have told Harper that Tilly forgot about meals because she needed so few calories herself, but she couldn't expect Harper, who needed a great deal of calories, to be sympathetic, so she kept her mouth shut.

"She told me to make lunch for myself. So that's what I'm doing," said Harper, going into the kitchen. "I'm going into the kitchen and making myself lunch."

"Maybe I'll make something to bring up to Penpen," Ratchet said. She had been waiting politely for Tilly to do this, but now realized that she probably wouldn't and Penpen would be hungry.

"Always the saint," Harper said but was apparently glad for company in the kitchen. She still had visions of someone walking in and accusing her of stealing food. "So what do you know how to make?" she asked, banging and leaving open all the cupboard doors. "Hey, there's no food in here."

"It's all in the pantry," said Ratchet, opening the door to the little room with its well-stocked shelves.

"I want something hefty. Like maybe a side of beef," said Harper, guffawing. They made eggs and took a tray up to Penpen, who was sitting up and feeling much better.

"Thank you, dears," she said. "I'll be on my feet in no time. Then we can resume our driving lessons." Ratchet looked over at Harper, who didn't say anything. Ratchet could read nothing from her expression.

After Penpen had eaten, the girls helped move her to her armchair by the window. She didn't need help walking, but Tilly said that you could be woozy from lying down all the time if you weren't used to it and that Harper and Ratchet should try to walk alongside Penpen if she appeared to be making any small journeys through the house.

"Of course," Tilly had said, "if she falls on you, all that will be left of you is an inkspot on the carpet." And then they knew that Tilly was feeling better, too.

It was a perfect summer day. They all gazed at it out the window. A hummingbird was hovering over the flowers in the small portion of the vegetable garden that Penpen allowed for cut flowers. "Oh my goodness, my garden! Has Tilly done any weeding?" asked Penpen in sudden horror.

Ratchet shook her head. "She's been busy with the bees."

"Oh yes, the bees," said Penpen. "Oh dear, and Dr Richardson isn't letting me do anything for the next two weeks. Not that I feel as if I could garden, but it's going to go to rack and ruin. We rely on it!"

"I don't know anything about gardening," Ratchet said. "I couldn't tell a weed from a vegetable."

"Oh, I know, I know, dear," said Penpen worriedly to herself. She hadn't even considered Ratchet. Her garden had been built with years of tender service. It needed an expert, as far as she was concerned. "Oh, this is a mess. I hate to ask Tilly."

Harper stood up and exploded, "Well, what about me? Christ! You're acting like I'm not even in the room!" She went stomping out.

Penpen and Ratchet watched her departing back in surprise. "Well, that was curious," said Penpen finally. "I wouldn't have thought her the gardening type."

But Harper was a gardener and a very good one, that is to say, a very conscientious gardener. The type that plods out steadily in all weathers and does the careful, knowledgeable, minute work that good gardens require. She had been taught well in the community gardens of Helox, where a family on subsistence income could rent a patch for ten dollars a season and receive the tutelage of an expert gardener who made daily rounds, going from plot to plot, assisting those who asked for it. In Harper's neighbourhood she was fortunate to have a small, wizened ex–Buddhist monk, a coincidence that Penpen would have found very exciting if Harper had told her, but Harper was still keeping the important things to herself. He had not at first pegged Harper as a gardener apt to last the whole season. Many people allotted the community plots started out with great garden plans, but when they found out how much work a good garden required, particularly in the challenging soil of the vacant lot chosen for the community plots, they fell off midspring, one by one. Mr Ziang didn't think Harper would last through the ploughing, not to mention the planting. But when he found her there midsummer and realized she was still faithfully tending a bumper crop of peas, he became interested and began to advise her.

The truth was that before the community garden came along, Harper wasn't getting any vegetables at all. Miss Madison couldn't understand why anyone would buy vegetables when they could get Cheetos. She had no time for them. She disliked anything she had to clean and cook. She was squeamish about cutting off broccoli stems, washing dirt off celery, peeling carrots. She thought potatoes in their raw form were disgusting and that lettuce was a leaf trap for bugs. She hated the way vegetables tasted and made the house stink when you cooked them. But Harper's little growing body knew it was missing something, and when she pulled up her first new carrot and chewed experimentally on it, she was hooked. Harper loved vegetables. After that, the garden became her own. Miss Madison thought she was crazy.

"What do you want to spend all your free time over there digging in some mud for?" she would ask, lying sideways on the armchair eating potato chips and drinking diet soda and watching talk shows on TV. But Harper regarded this as a rhetorical question and ignored it. She brought home buckets of vegetables as summer drifted on and ate them all alone in her room where Miss Madison couldn't complain about the mess or the dirt or the smell.

When she got her hands on Penpen's garden, after explaining to Penpen how much she did know and how Penpen had gone wrong in her planting, she knew just what she wanted to do. She tackled it with excitement, each new vegetable like a little solar system. She explored in greater depth what Penpen had done, what she had planted next to what, what measures she had taken to prevent root rot and bugs and other gardening disasters. She began to spend longer and longer hours out in the rows while Penpen watched from her window. Sometimes Penpen would wave down to her, but usually Harper was too absorbed to notice.

And so the next two weeks drifted on, Tilly, Harper, and Ratchet doing the work on the property. When Penpen got well enough to shuffle around the house, she went back to making the meals, which pleased them all, as, though they had been able to handle the bees, chickens, cow, and garden, no one had displayed any culinary talent or inclination, and when Tilly cooked dishes, there was usually something in them that shouldn't have been.

One night after dinner, when Harper was coming up from an evening dip in the sea, covered in sunburn from working in the garden all afternoon, Penpen called her into her room.

"Yeah?" said Harper.

"I want to give you a little present," said Penpen, getting up and shuffling toward her closet.

"Oh yeah?" said Harper looking interestedly toward Penpen's closet.

"It's this." Penpen took a big soft straw hat down. "They don't make them like this any more. I've worn this hat for sixty-some years in the garden. It's handmade. It will last for ever. My happiest moments have been putting on that hat in the morning and going down and, well, you know."

Harper knew exactly what Penpen was saying. She knew the moment in the morning when you first sank your hands into the soil. She knew the feeling of the sun-warmed earth, and the cool evening soil and the dry baking soil and the smell of rain on it. It was like putting your hand on the heart of the earth. It was like putting your hand on your own heart.

"You're all sunburnt. You need a hat," said Penpen. "I want to give you this one."

"You want to give me a hat?" said Harper, looking uncertain, as if she couldn't quite believe anyone would want to give her anything.

"Yes," said Penpen.

"Well, for Christ's sake, then," said Harper, "don't give me one that's sixty years old."

Harper thought of the hat sitting on someone's dandruffy, sweaty scalp for sixty years and shuddered.

Penpen started. Then she laughed. "Well, I haven't any new hats to give you," she said. Then she became outraged. "Besides, that's a perfectly fine hat! That's been my gardening hat for sixty years!"

"Exactly. Jeez! The hat I want is in an online catalogue. It's broad-brimmed and soft straw and costs twenty-nine dollars plus shipping and it hasn't been sitting on somebody's head for sixty years."

"But, Harper, I wouldn't even know where to get ahold of such a catalogue," said Penpen, distractedly putting her spurned hat away.

"On the Internet. How many times do I have to tell you that you can get anything off the Internet."

"But you know we don't have a computer."

"Well, I bet that Dr Richardson does. I bet he's got one. And you could order me the hat and also a swimsuit, if you wouldn't mind. They ship it and it gets to you in four to six days. With any luck it would arrive before Maddy takes me to Canada."

"Yes," said Penpen worriedly. When Harper started talking about Maddy taking her to Canada she got very worried because she had to think once again about what was likely to happen to Harper. If Miss Madison did take her, she might be dropped somewhere else on the road with other seemingly trustworthy people but who might not be as trustworthy as Penpen and Tilly. Or, as Tilly suspected, just dropped. Or maybe Miss Madison would make it all the way to St Cyr's this time, and Penpen didn't think St Cyr's was any place for a fourteen-year-old girl. On the other hand, how could she and Tilly continue to care for her, and what would happen to her when they stopped? How would Harper feel when Ratchet, the only other vital young thing in the house, left at the end of the summer? "Oh, Harper!" she said involuntarily.

"Well, what do you say? Can we at least drive in and ask him?"

The idea of driving anywhere was not very appealing to Penpen, but she always liked to see Dr Richardson. He had only been in to check on her once, but she supposed he got very busy in the woods this time of year. Those loggers always seemed to have trees and axes falling on them.

"He's supposed to be coming in soon," she said. "We can ask him then."

"Yes, but we can't use his computer if he comes here," said Harper.

"If he has a computer."

"I say we go to him," said Harper.

"I'll think about it," said Penpen. "And, of course, we would have to ask Tilly. She'd have to do all the driving."

"I'm taking that as a yes," said Harper and that night at dinner explained her plan to Tilly and Ratchet. Tilly needed her liquor supply refilled. She had been downing it a bit more heavily in the evenings since Penpen had taken ill. Ratchet dreaded a drive again since the last, but Tilly felt if they were going to go, they should all go, so the next day they set out.

Dr Richardson was at home having coffee and cookies with his wife on their porch when they arrived. He took Penpen inside immediately to examine her. Not only was Penpen doing splendidly, he announced, he did indeed own a computer. He was showing Tilly and Penpen how to use it when Harper took over. Her fingers had been itching for the Net.

"Well," said Dr Richardson, stepping aside, "I suppose the young are so much more adept than we old folks. They've been brought up to it."

"Oh, don't call yourself old," tittered Penpen.

Honestly, thought Tilly!

Ratchet stood in the background quietly watching Harper shop.

"You ought to get *her* –" Harper jerked a thumb back in Ratchet's direction – "a new swimsuit, too, instead of that baggy one that's all pinned everywhere. Oh, I forgot! That thing." Ratchet pulled her borrowed sweater more tightly around her shoulders and hunched over as if she hadn't heard but was fascinated by the computer.

"*Harper!*" said Tilly sharply.

"Oh, here we are, here we are, this one," said Harper. "And here's a hat. Let's put that in the shopping cart, too. Now all I need is your credit card number, postal box, and zip code."

"We haven't got a credit card," said Penpen.

Harper stopped and turned slowly to stare at them. "You haven't got a credit card? Even Maddy has a credit card and she hasn't got any credit. Why don't you have a credit card? How can you live without a credit card?"

"You can live without all kinds of silly things, you little twit," said Tilly. "It's not Penpen and I who feel the need to order things from computer catalogues. Why don't you tell them we'll send them a money order? Or a cheque? We do have cheques, don't we, Penpen?"

"Yes, of course, that's how I pay the electric, Tilly."

"But by the time you send out a cheque and the stuff is shipped, I'll be gone to *Canada*!" wailed Harper.

"Oh, here, use mine," said Dr Richardson irritably, whipping out his wallet. The sound of young women wailing wasn't one he heard often and he found it most annoying. He had known loggers pinned under trees who made less noise. "Tilly, you and Penpen can pay me back in cash. Credit cards!" He shook his head and wandered back to the porch to sit again with Mrs Richardson, who was quiet and didn't even crunch her cookies loudly. Tilly joined them. She had had enough of the modern world for one day.

After Harper had finished ordering her items, Penpen somewhat hesitantly asked Ratchet if there was anything she would like, and just as Penpen suspected, Ratchet looked so violently embarrassed at the idea of rudely asking for things the way Harper did that Penpen dropped it and scooted them out to the porch. They returned Dr Richardson's credit card and he put it swiftly back into his wallet as if he didn't even want to think of it. Mrs Richardson offered them cookies, but all except Harper felt they had imposed enough for one day and Tilly hustled them back to the car. On the way through town, Tilly said, "Oh, and I have to drop that damn quilt square off at Myrtle Trout's house. I really hope she's not home. I don't know about you, Penpen, but I feel I couldn't possibly come up with more small talk." Penpen nodded agreement. Nevertheless they were about to have more, for at that moment Miss Madison came waddling down the steps of the boarding house, intent on marching into town strictly against doctor's orders and buying more cigarettes. As they drove by at their usual stately pace, she spotted Harper and impulsively raced up to the car, crying, "HARPER! BABY!"

Tilly slammed on the brakes, which, since they had been going only ten miles an hour, merely brought them to a gentle stop, and Harper climbed out of the car. Miss Madison put her arms around Harper and said, "Oh, Harper, baby. I've missed you." Harper looked back at Tilly and Penpen as if to say, "What did I tell you?"

"So you haven't had that baby yet, huh, Maddy?" said Harper, eyeing Miss Madison's stomach, which was hanging low upon her legs.

"Naw, but that dumb doctor says it could come anytime."

Penpen bristled at this slur on Dr Richardson, but she withheld comment.

"Anyhow, it's time for you to come home, girl," said Miss Madison. "I'm sorry I got sore about the swimsuit."

"Sure," said Harper. "What do I need a swimsuit for anyhow?"

"That's what I was trying to tell you. But sheesh, now your stuff's all at that place in the woods, huh? What do they call it?"

"Glen Rosa," said Tilly coldly.

"Right." Miss Madison looked at Tilly and Penpen through narrowed eyes as if they hardly existed. "How about you folks, seeing as how my condition's delicate and all, drive Harper's stuff over to us when you get the chance? I mean, she can wear what she's wearing for a day or two, so like, no big rush."

"Now listen," began Tilly in an irritable voice, "we've got a delicate condition of our own here." But Penpen put a hand on Tilly's forearm, which still hung on the steering wheel as if she were ready to step on the gas and whisk Harper away if she changed her mind about returning to Miss Madison.

"We'd be happy to," said Penpen. "We'd be happy to do whatever Harper wants. Is that what you want, Harper?"

"My clothes?" asked Harper in confusion. She was not reading the subtexts, but Penpen later explained to Tilly that she had thought it was time she suggest to Miss Madison that maybe *someone* ought to think about what was best for Harper.

"Yes, shall we bring them back?"

"Well, I gotta wear something. I can't go around like a buck-naked wild man," said Harper and ran up the steps to the boarding house without a backward glance, as if Miss Madison might change her mind at any moment.

"There she goes and I was just going to ask her to go into town and get those cigarettes for me. Oh well, I'll catch her inside," said Miss Madison to thin air, because it had also occurred to Tilly that Miss Madison might suddenly change her mind and start buffeting Harper about again and she decided to pull away from the kerb before Miss Madison could do that to Harper.

They were silent in the Daimler until they got to the turn-off to Glen Rosa. Then Tilly said, "I wouldn't go around cancelling any catalogue orders just yet, that's all I have to say."

Penpen nodded grimly as a bear ran across the road. "Goddamn bears."

"Goddamn bears," agreed Tilly.

HARPER TWO

When they pulled into the yard, Ratchet could hear the phone ringing. She ran in to get it while Tilly and Penpen eased themselves slowly out of the car. Neither was strong enough any more to help the other.

"Hello, Ratchet?" said Henriette.

"Mom!" said Ratchet. It had been weeks since she had heard from Henriette.

"Where were you? I've been phoning all day."

"We drove into town. Penpen had a heart attack. Not today, but—"

"Penpen had a heart attack? How do you know? Lots of people think they have heart attacks when it's only indigestion."

"Dr Richardson said it was a heart attack."

"Humph. Is she in the hospital?"

"No, she doesn't like hospitals. Neither does Tilly."

"Then it couldn't have been a heart attack."

"Well, Penpen says Dr Richardson is a very good doctor. But anyhow she's doing fine now and we went to his house and did some online shopping."

"Is she buying you more stuff without asking me? Lot of fun spending someone else's money. Wish I could."

"It wasn't for me. It was for Harper."

"Who is Harper?"

"Her mother got lost going to the orphanage at St Cyr's and ended up here and Penpen and Tilly took her in but her Aunt Maddy keeps changing her mind about whether she can keep her or not and when we were in town we ran into Miss Madison and she took her back."

"I can't follow any of this, Ratchet. It sounds demented. If they're going to take in boarders they'd better vet them first. Who knows who they could end up with. Robbers. Murderers. Anyhow, that's not why I called. I called because Hutch and I are coming to visit. Hutch is the tennis pro at the Hunt Club."

Ratchet's mouth went dry. She wanted to ask if Hutch was the boyfriend. She figured he was, but she wanted to know for sure.

"Hutch is very nice, Ratchet, and he plays tennis like a pro." Her mother burst into laughter as it suddenly occurred to her that she had made a joke. "He's even going to try to help me become a member. Of course, we can't really afford a membership, but all things come to those who wait. Anyhow, the best time for us to come is week after next because Hutch has his vacation. He wants to see the Maine coast. He thought it was a great coincidence that

that is where Penpen and Tilly live. We won't be able to stay long because the prattle will undoubtedly get to us. Oh, and Hutch says he wants to meet you."

Ratchet nodded silently.

"Speak up, Ratchet. Better yet, put Penpen or Tilly on the phone. Whichever one seems to have more of her marbles at the moment. I have to make arrangements. And listen, Ratchet, I know I don't need to tell you that it's going to be very important, *very* important, to keep That Thing covered when Hutch is there. He doesn't like infirmities. Even little ones like warts and grey hairs and things. He keeps himself in very, very good shape. He gets *French manicures*. How many men do you know who would bother with that? There's nothing we can do about sprucing up Penpen and Tilly, I suppose, but it doesn't matter anyway because they won't really have any bearing on things."

Tilly was coming through the door, so Ratchet called out to her and handed her the phone.

Later Penpen, Ratchet, and Tilly were sitting around the kitchen table having a supper of soft-boiled eggs when Ratchet finally spoke. "I suppose she didn't say so specifically, but I suppose that Hutch is the boyfriend."

"I'm surprised, frankly," said Tilly, taking a bite of egg. The trip into town had given her an unusual appetite. "Because I would have thought she'd make a beeline for someone with a little more money. Tennis pros can't make all that much."

Penpen put down her spoon and looked shocked. "Tilly, really! And after all, perhaps she's in love. Love knows no bank statements."

142

"He's promised to help her get into the Hunt Club," said Ratchet. "And she says he's pretty physically perfect."

"Of course, people get married for all kinds of reasons. Look at me," said Tilly. "So I guess Henriette is entitled to her own reasons."

"Did they say they were getting married?" asked Penpen.

"Not in so many words," said Tilly mysteriously.

"In any words?"

"Well, no," admitted Tilly reluctantly.

"Well, I guess we'll find out when they get here. So, they're flying into Bangor and renting a car?" said Penpen.

"Yes. Perhaps they'll take the wrong turn-off from Dink," said Tilly hopefully.

"Tilly!" said Penpen.

"People do," said Tilly innocently, cracking open another egg.

"Tilly, please," said Penpen.

But she needn't have. Ratchet felt the same way. She was having mixed feelings about Hutch. That night as she sat in her window seat looking down toward the sea she realized that part of her was relieved at the idea of Hutch. Hutch might take on some of the responsibility for her mother's happiness. She just didn't know where she would fit into the threesome, and if Hutch didn't like her, she had a feeling she wouldn't fit in at all, and then what? Or if Hutch disliked her so much that he left Henriette, then Ratchet would be wholly responsible for ruining her mother's shot at happiness. She began to understand how Harper must feel, not knowing what was going to happen to her. It gave her a restless energy as though she couldn't quite settle down to anything. As if moving around a lot without thinking were the best idea.

A couple of days later the doorbell rang and Tilly and Penpen, who were reading in the parlour, stopped and looked at each other.

"You know, Tilly," said Penpen, "I'm beginning to get used to people coming to the door. For years not a soul showed up and then Ratchet arrives and suddenly it's Grand Central Station."

"Humph," said Tilly, who would never get used to it. She didn't like anyone interrupting her plans. Even when she didn't have plans, she didn't want her unplannedness interrupted. "You know, if Father had really wanted to isolate Mother, he should have fixed the phone so no one could call in. Or he should have removed it altogether. . ." she began, and then suddenly she and Penpen had the same thought. "Harper!" they cried and got up, shuffling quickly to the door. But it wasn't Harper. It was Myrtle Trout, looking very put out.

"I hear you had a heart attack," she said, charging into the room and giving Penpen a big bouquet of daisies that had a bee in it. Later on, when the bee had been finally killed after a long day of Tilly and Ratchet chasing it around the house, Penpen said to Tilly, "You know, I bet she picked those daisies from the side of the road on the way in. They didn't look cut. They had the mangled look of the picked bouquet. And to think she'd get out of that car with her terror of the bears." And Tilly replied, "Well, there you go, cheapness will take you where terror won't. Human beings are amazing."

"I'm not surprised to see you laid up," Myrtle continued. "Serves you right for taking in two young girls, one of them de-formed." She said it as if it were two words, as if all of them were formed and Ratchet was the anti-form. Ratchet, who was in the kitchen washing out blueberry jars, shuddered at the thought.

"What is it, Myrtle?" snapped Tilly, shuffling more slowly back. She was getting tireder and tireder, she thought, as she gently settled herself on the old velvet love seat. Even a little trip across the room was exhausting her. But I mustn't be so tired, she thought worriedly, not until the end of the summer, when Ratchet has gone and Penpen has had a chance to catch up. She's a good many heart attacks behind.

"Would you like some tea?" asked Penpen, hoping Myrtle would say no because she knew neither she nor Tilly had the wherewithal right now to fetch it and she didn't want to ask Ratchet. But when Myrtle said yes, and sat calmly poised, her hands folded in her lap, waiting in happy expectancy for a cookie, Penpen had no choice but to call Ratchet and ask her if she couldn't just kindly brew up a pot of tea and bring a few cookies from the jar.

Ratchet came in with everything on a tray, walking carefully with the heavy, cumbersome burden, trying not to slop anything on to the cookie plate. She put the tray down gently on the coffee table and handed around the cups with a cookie on each saucer.

"There, dear, thank you," said Myrtle, giving her a crocodile smile.

So insincere, sniffed Tilly to herself. If she were younger and fitter she'd hobble over there and give that Myrtle Trout a good swift kick in the shins.

"There now," Myrtle said, sighing complacently, the sigh somehow going right into her big belly and shifting her fat around the chair. It wasn't that Myrtle was so fat particularly, thought Penpen, and certainly most women as old as Myrtle Trout, Tilly excepted, had long ago lost a waistline. No, it was just that she was so *loose*, the flesh moving about like a bunch of basketballs piled in a net. Penpen was aggrieved to find herself staring at Myrtle, who was staring at Ratchet as she served the tea, trying to get a glimpse of that thing through Ratchet's clothes. This was the real reason she had come. She had never seen anything like it before, she couldn't tell Burl exactly what it was, was it a growth, or a mole, or some kind of deformed bone? She hated not to be able to tell him precisely, and she longed to see it again.

"Well," she said, "that's all the news and then the sports. I see you have nothing to add, living all the way out here and never getting into town."

Ratchet almost said, We were just recently in town. But why open that kettle of fish, she thought and returned to the kitchen.

"Well . . . the quilt square?" said Myrtle finally.

"Oh dang," said Tilly. "It's in the car. I meant to drop it off the other day, but we ran into Miss Madison, and Harper jumped ship, which reminds me, Myrtle, your visit is, for once, very well timed. Would you mind taking Harper's things to her? I said I would drive them in, but you may as well if you're headed in that direction anyhow."

"Oh my, what's the point? By now I imagine those two are

halfway to Canada," said Myrtle. "Why don't you keep the clothes for Ratchet? She might like something that hasn't been made out of spit and safety pins."

"Her mother's coming to visit soon. She'll bring her real clothes," snapped Tilly. She was offended that someone would criticize the clothes they had creatively provided for Ratchet and annoyed again at the thought of Henriette's forgetting to send Ratchet with a suitcase. "And anyhow, are you suggesting we just keep Harper's things like some kind of . . . some kind of . . . grave robber?"

"Grave robber, my foot. Now, there's a cat that will always land on its paws. I ran into her a couple of days ago at the store buying her aunt cigarettes, and when I said that I thought it was a disgrace, her being sent out with the cigarette money like that, she said, why, she was the one going to smoke them, and then she went out on the porch and lit up just to show me, but let me tell you, I made that child smoke that cigarette clean to the filter. I stood there and watched her, daring her to follow up on her big brag, and if that child was a smoker, then I'm a monkey's uncle. Hawking and choking! There now, don't play games with me again, sister, I said to myself."

"Honestly, Myrtle, you mean you made her smoke that cigarette to the end just to spite her? A parentless fourteen-year-old girl? What's gotten into you? Or rather, what was in you to begin with and why don't you get rid of it?" snapped Tilly.

"Nonsense. I tell you, I had twelve of my own and I know how to deal with them. The voice of experience never bothers to debate with the. . ." Myrtle couldn't think what the antithesis of the voice of experience was, so she finally blurted out, "crazy old harpies who shut themselves up in the woods."

"Dear, dear," said Penpen, folding and unfolding her hands. "Dear, dear."

"And what do you mean, they're halfway to Canada?" demanded Tilly suddenly.

"The BABY!" said Myrtle. "I forgot to tell you, the woman had the BABY. Well, she'd been telling everyone in town for days and days that the second that little brat poked its head out she was hitting the road, so I guess she took Harper and that baby and split."

"She had the baby?" repeated Penpen faintly. She felt an odd crush of disappointment at the thought of the whole business finished and done with and Harper on the road, even though she suspected it was what Harper wanted.

"Yeah, huh?" said Myrtle happily. "Had it at ten-fifteen night before last. Came mighty fast for a first baby is what some of us think, if you know what we mean. Anyhow, Dr Richardson said that she was further along than anyone had suspected and the baby wasn't premature or anything. Perfectly healthy bouncing baby girl. Named Harpertu."

"Harper two?" said Tilly.

"Harper too?" said Penpen.

"Harpertu," said Myrtle, and no one understood what the others had said but all thought they were repeating the same thing.

"Well, I must be off. I'll just collect that quilt square on my way out."

"Wait a second," said Tilly. "I want to get Harper's things. Surely she isn't on the road yet. Dr Richardson wouldn't let Miss Madison leave so soon after having a baby."

"Dr Richardson's got nothing to say about it. Do you know that that woman gave birth, I mean literally pushed that baby out, with a *cigarette* stuck between her teeth? Mrs Richardson, who assisted at the birth, said that she clamped right down on the filter and twice broke right through it during the pains, but they had to keep giving her fresh ones because she said she wouldn't push if she didn't have a smoke. It's bad enough having the pain, she said, she wasn't going to suffer through nicotine withdrawal, too."

"What did Dr Richardson say?" asked Penpen, who frankly doubted this whole story. People *would* talk.

"Well, you know him," said Myrtle in disgust. "He never does anything about anything. You know he let that old logger who had the tree fall on him die right out there in the woods."

Both Tilly and Penpen were familiar with the indignation this story aroused. It happened many years before, a logger who chose dying pinned under a tree to being saved and losing his legs. Dr Richardson claimed there was nothing he could do to save him, but everyone pretty much knew he could have. "What's a legless logger supposed to do?" Penpen had asked at the time.

"Anyhow, bet those two are long gone," said Myrtle.

"Well, do me a favour and take the suitcase over to the boarding house anyway," said Tilly, bringing it downstairs. "Just in case."

"I will not, Tilly Menuto. What do I want to be hauling away an

149

old thing like that in my nice clean car anyway? It's probably crawling with cooties," said Myrtle, eyeing it with distaste. "You go giving it to the poor the next time you're in town if you like. I'm not bringing it back with me. I'm not. Oh well, hand it over. Foolish waste of time. Maybe I'll get Burl to do it. I have a hundred errands of my own and this quilt piecing to do." Myrtle grabbed the suitcase and tromped down the stone path to her car, getting a heel caught in the stones and tripping. She could usually be counted on to do the right thing in the end, but she was exasperated by constantly coming up against this quality in herself. "I hope you did a nice job with that square. It would be so awful if you didn't because everyone else has done such lovely work and we don't want it to stand out."

Tilly looked at her and slammed the front door as hard as she could, but it unfortunately only creaked shut. "Damned infirmities. Damned age. And damned old fool," she said.

"Tilly," said Penpen.

"Well, honestly, Penpen, who wears high heels in the woods? It's . . . it's like making a *show* of stupidity."

Penpen knew Tilly was too upset for it to have been just Myrtle pressing her buttons. Myrtle wasn't worth the energy. She suspected that Tilly, too, was disappointed to hear of Harper's leaving town with finality. But she needn't have been, because the next morning while Ratchet was still milking the cow, before the sun had even completely risen and as the edges of the sky glowed peach and red, Miss Madison, Harper, and Harpertu appeared on the doorstep, grim and unsmiling.

THAT THING

"Harper!" said Tilly before she had a chance to moderate her enthusiasm for this obnoxious but strangely compelling child. She had gotten up to answer the door, but at her cry Penpen and Ratchet came to the door as well. They all stood around looking awkwardly at Miss Madison, who stood grim and determined with an unusually quiet Harper, hands knuckled white, clenching the handle of her beat-up suitcase by the door.

"I gave Harper this suitcase," said Miss Madison defensively. "It was the only one I've ever had. It belonged to my mother. I'm keeping my stuff and the baby's in some cartons." She hefted the baby, who was so tightly swaddled that they couldn't see her, closer to her breast, shifting its weight unconsciously as if it were still part of her body, attached to her arms instead of her belly, attached to her in a way Harper would never be.

"I told her she can keep it. The thing is, it's not going to work out, her coming with me to Canada. I can see that now. This little baby, well, she's Pierre's, that's the name of her father, she's his child, and the grandmother's got to have a feeling for that if I can find her. But it kind of weakens our case, you know, if I show up with a bunch of bastards in tow. I don't mean that in a bad way, but let's face it, neither of these kids enjoyed the benefit of their parents' wedlock exactly. She probably won't even believe that Harper's not mine."

Penpen, who was the only one to respond, nodded as sympathetically as she could. No one looked at Harper.

"I named her Harpertu, anyhow, so as to remember Harper."

"How nice," said Penpen hastily because it looked as if Harper was about to cry and didn't want to. "Harper, why don't you go in and have some breakfast?"

"No, I'll just stay here until they go," said Harper, not moving, not releasing the grip on the suitcase, and not looking at anyone.

"Can I see little Harper?" said Penpen because truthfully none of them knew what to say. It occurred to Ratchet that if Miss Madison was going to go she ought to just go quickly.

For a second Miss Madison's face lit up as she uncovered Harpertu's face. "It's Harper*tu*," she said.

"Harper too?" asked Penpen.

"Yeah, Harpertu. H-a-r-p-e-r-t-u. I liked it. Had kind of a foreign ring about it. It'll be kind of an exotic name to take up there to French Canada. And like I said, I wanted to do something kind of to remember Harper by because if I could've seen a way to, I would have taken her, too. She knows that, don't you, Harper?"

"Yeah, I know," said Harper.

"And I guess Dr Richardson said it's OK for you to travel, did he?" said Penpen.

"Oh, sure, he said I was made to drop babies like some kind of peasant woman in the field. That he never saw such an easy birth. He said I could have a whole slew of them. Not that I'm gonna. Well, look, I guess I better go. It's OK if I leave Harper here? I mean, you can always take her the rest of the way to St Cyr's if you change your mind."

"That won't be necessary," said Tilly tersely. It was the first time she had spoken. Miss Madison turned to her and her face hardened.

"Yeah, well, sometimes there aren't no good decisions," said Miss Madison. "And Harper knows that." She turned and went down the porch steps, hugging her baby close to her. Harper watched while she put the baby into its infant seat, carefully backed up, and turned the car. Miss Madison never looked at the porch again. After she drove away, Harper sat down on the porch steps next to her suitcase and, as the morning went on, slowly relinquished her grasp on it.

For the next few days Penpen tried to get Harper into the garden, but Harper didn't seem interested in much of anything.

"Well, you can hardly blame her," said Tilly to Penpen and Ratchet. They were all sitting on the porch shelling peas in the perfect summer weather. "To get dumped by both your mother and the woman who effectively became your mother. And I think right up to the end she probably thought that woman was going to come back and get her. She'd changed her mind so many times before. Penpen, you're getting empty pods all over the porch."

Penpen looked down and kicked them off the porch absent-mindedly. "I'm thinking she must feel so exposed, us seeing her being dumped. I ought to tell her about finding Mother's head."

"Oh God, Penpen, nobody needs that story. That's just dreadful."

"You found your mother's head?" said Ratchet.

"Penpen, don't you dare tell that story. It's not the type of story that would make anyone feel better. All it will do is give the girls nightmares."

"Well, I just hate to think of that child wandering around the property feeling so alone."

"Well, fine, but for heaven's sake, don't tell *that* story," said Tilly and closed her eyes and fell asleep. Tilly was taking a lot of naps lately, as if it were too exhausting to remain conscious for long.

Harper drifted in silently for meals, which were finally a regular feature at Glen Rosa. But she had lost her interest in eating everyone else's dessert. She wouldn't garden. And she didn't seem interested in conversation, so they were all surprised one night after dinner when out of nowhere she said, "What is that thing on your shoulder blade, anyway?"

Tilly, who was slumped halfway on the table with her sherry glass two inches from her nose, lifted her eyes and said halfheartedly, "*Harper!*"

"I was born with it," said Ratchet.

"It's nobody's business," said Tilly.

"My mother says that it made the doctors scream when I was born but they all assured her it might spontaneously disappear. That babies are born with all kinds of horrible things that just drop off in time. One paediatrician suggested that we cover it up until it did."

"Why didn't your mother just have it removed?" said Harper, crunching on the leftover raspberry crumble. "That's what I would have done. What's the big deal? What kind of a dimwit goes around covering up her kid's birthmark when she can just have it taken off?"

Tilly would have objected, but her head was on the table and she was asleep.

"Shush, girls," said Penpen, gesturing to Tilly. "Asleep."

"Or passed out," said Harper in disgust, moving the sherry decanter back to the liquor cabinet. "She has pretty high old times for such an old broad."

Penpen made tsking noises. She couldn't decide whether she should object to this truthful observation or not.

"Why don't you get Dr Richardson to remove it. He can remove stuff, right?" said Harper.

"Well, he did remove Guy Dion's leg," said Penpen thoughtfully.

"There you go," said Harper, sounding almost cheerful again.

"And Caspar Vendetti's right fingers."

"I'm sure fingers are harder to take off than that thing," said Harper.

"We could do it as a surprise for my mother. Before she gets here," said Ratchet.

"Are you sure you want to bother removing it at all, dear?" asked Penpen as Ratchet and Harper cleared the dinner plates and began washing the dishes.

But Ratchet was daydreaming. She had visions of herself and Hutch and her mother at the Hunt Club having lunch, swimming in the club pool, just a tiny butterfly-shaped scar on her shoulder blade. "I could pay you back someday. I'd sign an IOU."

"No, no," said Penpen rapidly, "I certainly didn't mean that." Something about this worried her, and it wasn't until she got into bed that she realized where her nebulous fears came from. The next morning she got up and sat on the hammock watching Harper, who she was glad to see was at least beginning to garden again. No matter what, Harper would never be able to stay out of a garden for long. Ratchet hadn't yet come in from the barn. "You know," said Penpen, "I don't know if we should encourage Ratchet to get that thing removed."

"Well, it's your nickel," said Harper, getting tough on the weeds that had accumulated in her absence.

"You know, it wasn't too far from here, where we used to have a lovely little gazebo, that I found my mother's head."

Harper stopped.

"Yes, yes," said Penpen, vigorously nodding in response to Harper's look of shocked disbelief. "You might wonder what would be worse, I certainly have over the years, finding just the body, or just the head, or the head and body together, well – not together – they were certainly apart – irreparably, you might say – but in the same general vicinity, as opposed to the unnatural state of one without the other, which is what happened. In fact, come to think of it, saying it that way, it does clarify it for me, it would have been much better if the body had been alongside it. But it wasn't. No, it was just the head I came upon. I had been skipping. I was really too old to skip, but living out here with only the servants to see me, I often did anyway, around and around the garden and up and down the garden paths. We used to have much better gardens, Harper. And many of them. You would have loved them. Of course, we had gardeners. You simply can't have those kinds of extensive gardens without gardeners."

"Don't I know it," said Harper.

"Well, I'm skipping along, thinking nothing very interesting ever happens to me. And that's when I saw the hair. It was matted with blood, of course. You can't chop off your own head without getting your hair all soaked."

"Kind of like a last shampoo," said Harper.

"Hmm," said Penpen. She was thinking that when Harper was allowed to just be in the garden she was a different person. Softer, somehow. "Yes. So I naturally stop."

"Naturally. I also brake for heads," said Harper.

"And I think to myself, and I'll never forget this, I wonder what Mother's head is doing in the garden?"

"You were probably in shock," said Harper.

"Exactly. But at the time I am thinking to myself that isn't it odd that I am thinking these thoughts quite rationally when really I should be screaming something incoherently. Oh well, you can't help how you are in a crisis."

"Once Maddy found a black widow spider in the bathroom. She beat it to death with a pan and broke four tiles. The landlord made her pay for them, too, and she said she would sue him for keeping poisonous insects in his building. But I'll never forget watching her beating and beating that spider with the pan long after it was dead. She was like, just *mad* at it for being there, you know? That's what she told me later when I said, you know you were hitting that thing long after it had the living daylights smushed out of it, and she said, yeah, but she was mad at it, mad at it for being there, mad at it for the way things always turn out, mad at that crummy little hovel we lived in with its ugly tiles. Mad that there don't ever seem to be any men around when you need them. I never saw her lose it like that again, but I remember thinking that I was glad when she finally got mad it was at that spider and not at me. So what did your mother use to cut off her head?"

"Oh, she rigged a series of pulleys and a chopping block made out of a stone garden bench that she could kneel in front of and she used an axe. She took the blade off the handle and attached it to a rope. A kind of makeshift guillotine. It was quite elaborate. I imagine she must have been working on the plans for it for some time."

"Why didn't she just get herself a gun?"

"I don't know. I thought about that for years. We had guns around, so why choose such an elaborate and horrible and unreliable way? That's what struck me, the unreliability. Father and the coroner were talking later and he said that she must have had several tries that hadn't worked before she managed it, judging by the marks on the garden bench where the axe had hit. It must have come down and missed several times. Can you imagine what that must have been like? Knowing you'd missed and would have to gird yourself for your last minute all over again. Maybe this time chicken out? Maybe that's what she wanted. To have a way that would allow her to chicken out. To see if that's what she really wanted, after all."

"I guess it was," said Harper.

"Yes, I guess it was."

"Did she know that you skipped around the garden? That you might come across her?"

"The last few weeks we hardly saw her. She was so withdrawn. I didn't think of her as withdrawn back then. I was a teenager. I just knew she wasn't coming around for meals any more and would just, you know, pat me in passing. Of course, I knew something was wrong. I guess Tilly and I tried not to think about it. I guess probably that's why I was doing all that skipping to begin with. But we didn't talk about it. Not to her. Not to each other. Anyhow, there was her head. For years I dreamt that I picked it up and put it back on her body. But that wasn't my decision to make."

Tilly called to them from the porch, "It's noon!"

Penpen went in to make lunch, and then they drove into Dink to see Dr Richardson. He met them on the porch and led Penpen into his examining room first. Her worries about the wisdom of Ratchet's removing that thing were coalescing.

"You don't look well. Your colour's bad," said Dr Richardson.

"Well. . ." said Penpen.

"Are you *resting*?" he barked.

"I'm resting, but, Dan. . ." Penpen told Dr Richardson worriedly about what Ratchet wanted done.

"I'll have a look," he said. "So, if you've been getting so much rest, why do you look so worn out? Are the girls too much for you?"

"They're not too much now, Dan," said Penpen tiredly, "but I worry about what's to be. You've seen Tilly?"

Dr Richardson nodded glumly.

"And you know I'm not too far behind."

"Well, no way of predicting you, I'd say. You could be around for years. Depends. But I'd agree that for Tilly, time is limited."

"Yes, I know, it's what you warned us about a while back. She's getting thinner and tireder and her ankles and legs are swelling. It's congestive now. And I worry about finding a mother for Harper."

"Mother. Bah. That Harper's mother was one hard-bitten character. Harper's better off where she is with you and Tilly. She'd be better off at St Cyr's. Hell, she'd be better off with the bears."

"Oh, you can't believe that. Nobody's better off at an orphanage, surely. I don't know what to do with her is the thing."

"Well, you'll cross that bridge when you come to it. You don't want to bounce her too quickly someplace new anyhow. I'd say she needs a little rest. A little stability."

"Yes, but, Dan, even if she stayed the winter with us, where would we send her to school?"

"Home-school. You home-schooled."

"We had tutors."

"Lots of people home-school without tutors. Get yourself a

computer and get that damn phone line fixed."

"Oh, we couldn't do that. Tilly would never stand for it. She doesn't even like being able to take calls in. She likes leaving everything just as it was when Mother died. And Tilly's drinking more and more sherry. The last time we came into town she bought a case. I'm thinking of hiding it. It can't be good for her in her condition, can it?"

"No," said Dr Richardson.

"Should I take it away?"

Dr Richardson ran his hands through his hair and then said gently, "At this point I'd give her anything she wants, Pen."

Penpen started to cry. It took a while for her to pull herself together, and Dr Richardson passed her Kleenexes and looked grim. Sometimes it wasn't any fun to be a doctor. When she had finally stopped, and rinsed her face with wet paper towels until she lost her blotchy look, he said, "Send Ratchet in here and I'll see what I can do, if anything."

Ratchet was excited at the idea of That Thing being gone, but she wasn't too thrilled about the procedure. Dr Richardson gave her so many shots that she could feel no pain, but she could still feel what was being *done*. She was glad that he was chatty because if she had had to think of the movement of the scalpel against flesh and bone, she was certain she would have thrown up or fainted or both.

"So, you come from Florida, do you?" he asked cheerfully, going about the business as if he were baking a cake.

"Uh-huh," she said. She was afraid if she talked too much she would move and he would accidentally slice right into her liver.

"What part?"

"Pensacola."

"Pensacola . . . Pensacola . . . don't know anything about Pensacola. Feel I should know something about Pensacola. What can you tell me about Pensacola?"

"I don't really know anything about it either," said Ratchet, who was breathing shallowly and feeling a bit ill, what little she ever knew about Pensacola having temporarily left her brain.

"The wife and I want to retire to Florida. Wanted to for years."

"I thought you liked the woods!" Ratchet blurted out in astonishment. It seemed to surprise Dr Richardson either that she knew this or that she would blurt anything out.

"I do," he said, looking more kindly upon her but working steadily ahead. "I do. But the Mrs doesn't. She's put up with this place under the trees for our whole married life because, well, because there was a time when that's what women did, went where their husbands' work took them. And she never complained either. But the cold isn't good for Bertha. She doesn't like it and it gets in her bones. I'd like to take her somewhere warm for retirement. After all, we could come back here in the summers, couldn't we?"

"Uh-huh," said Ratchet, who could feel tugging and snipping at her flesh.

"Gets pretty hot there in the summer, I hear?"

"Uh-huh," said Ratchet again as flesh was pulled together and snipped some more. She thought of the cool blue pool of the Hunt Club. Thank God for the Hunt Club, she thought. Snip snip. Dr Richardson was scraping something again. Yes, the Hunt Club.

Thank God for that. A needle poked. What could he be doing? Yes. Where would we be without it? She felt the thread and the suturing of flesh. Right. Nowhere, that's where. Something wet being dabbed on. Well, thank God for it. She felt him snipping again. Yes, that's for sure. Her eyesight began to blur.

"Just hang on there a minute, then we'll put your head down," said Dr Richardson, who had had a lot of experience with people fainting, although usually it was big loggers who were watching their feet being amputated. Still, a faint was a faint, he thought. Not a very pleasant business.

"Yep," he went on rapidly and cheerfully, "that's where we'll go one day, but I gotta find a young doctor willing to take on the practice here first. Can't leave all these people to sew themselves up, deliver their own babies, write their own prescriptions, although by now most of them could. Every spring I send letters to the graduating classes of medical schools, and every year I fling the net farther and farther. Ready-made practice in the woods. Not a taker."

"How come?" asked Ratchet, who wasn't paying much attention but didn't want the chatter to stop. She kept thinking, Don't faint, don't faint, don't faint, like a mantra over and over.

"Not enough money. Most people seem to think making money is important to their survival. It's funny, when I came out here I never thought about that. I was thinking about making a life. I think medicine's an art. You have to learn to find things, a distortion, a feeling. . . It took me a lifetime to learn. I'm still learning. I still want to learn. What about you, huh?" When

Ratchet didn't answer he barked, "Huh?"

"Yes," she said, trying to answer without moving her lips. They were at a point where she really did not want to move. She felt as if her back had been carved wide open. She was afraid major organs would fall out if she moved.

"When I took up practising medicine it was because that's what I wanted to do, *practise medicine.* It wasn't so that I could make a lot of money and buy fancy things to put around a fancy house. Oh well, I came here because I wanted to and I wouldn't want any other person to come for any other reason. Take that aunt of yours. She knows what she wants. What feeds her. She wants to stay in the woods. Huh?"

"Tilly?" said Ratchet.

"No, not Tilly. Penpen. Penpen with her bees and the cow and the garden. It's Penpen who loves that old place."

"Right," said Ratchet. She would have said yes to anything. She was in a desperate panic, thinking, Please close me up, please close me up, please hurry. But through her panic, creeping like a warm river was the thought that she and Penpen had this in common. There was something about drifting through the misty light, moving from the quiet of the barn to the quiet of the hives, being in the middle of something.

"Right. And lots of folks think they're mad as hatters, that pair. But they've probably done what suits them. So anyhow, Bertha and I are waiting for someone to come forward who wants a life in the woods, same as I did, and wants to practise medicine. There, you're done. Wait a second, don't move, I'm going to give you a lollipop for not fainting. You needn't be insulted either, I give them to the loggers, too, and I've yet to see one refuse." He turned around to get it and that's when Ratchet fainted. But when she came to, he gave her the lollipop anyway. He said you also got one for coming to.

Ratchet was sore. It had not been as easy removing That Thing as they had hoped. She was taking antibiotics and codeine and lying in bed. Harper was happy. Her garden hat and swimsuit had come in. Tilly came down to the beach with her and Harper would push her back up the hill in the wheelbarrow. She was in the middle of unloading Tilly from one such trip when they heard a cry and, looking up, they saw a woman and a very bald younger man ascend from a car. "Oh, look," said the woman gaily as if this were a circus she had managed to find for the man's amusement, "it's Tilly in the wheelbarrow!" If Harper had remembered that Ratchet's mother was due to arrive she would have put two and two together and regarded her with curiosity, but she had forgotten and, taking one look at the woman, knew this was someone best avoided and went around to the back of the house to look for Penpen.

Tilly got out and squinted at the pair. She was always exhausted after her beach excursions and she wasn't happy to find strangers appearing in her yard. She hadn't seen Henriette since she was a girl and didn't recognize her, and all the excitement of Harper's return, Penpen's heart attack, and Ratchet's surgery, even though the surgery had been done *for* Henriette, had put Henriette's impending visit right out of her mind. Therefore when she went

165

charging up to them, at least at the turtle pace at which she could still charge, and pointed a bony finger, saying, "Who the hell are you?" Henriette merely thought she had gone completely off her rocker, which coincided nicely with what she had prepared Hutch for.

Hutch bounded forward in his best tennis bounce, moving lightly on the balls of his feet, as if preparing for a backhand swing at any moment. "Howdya do? Howdya do?" he garbled as he garbled most things when he was nervous, so that only random syllables escaped, giving the impression of someone trying to talk underwater with a mouthful of marbles.

"Get your hand away from me," snapped Tilly, slapping at it with her towel.

"Aunt Tilly, darling, this is Henriette," said Henriette slowly and carefully but keeping out of range of the towel, "come to visit again. You remember me."

Tilly gave her a long, hard look as if she suddenly recognized her but wished she didn't. She had hated the summers that Henriette had spent with them and had been very glad when she had outgrown the custom. She would have spit on Henriette, but Henriette was Ratchet's mother and she was very fond of Ratchet. "Oh, it's you," she said shortly. She turned to Hutch. "And I suppose you're the boyfriend?"

Hutch garbled something no one could understand. What he tried to say was, "Hutch, the name's Hutch."

"Well, come on up to the house if you must," said Tilly. "Ratchet is around here somewhere. I assume you intend to stay a few nights?"

"Don't want to be any trouble," said Hutch, but all that could be heard was "rant ny rouble" and Tilly was about to ask him politely to spit out whatever was in his mouth when there was a glad cry and Ratchet came running down the steps toward her mother. She stopped a few feet away and smiled shyly.

"Ratchet," said her mother. "Well, that was well timed. Ratchet, this is Hutch."

"Hyrda doo," mumbled Hutch, bounding up to shake her hand. "Awfully good little piece of land. Rather a lot of bears. Any tennis about?" He tried valiantly to make himself understood but knew he hadn't.

"Come in and have tea. I'm sure Penpen will want to serve you some," said Tilly and she stomped into the house. She insisted on taking tea in her swimsuit. She knew they were the type of people who would be disgusted by the body of a ninety-one-year-old woman. Hutch kept looking at it, but it was hard to tell from his expression whether he was fascinated or repelled.

Penpen had come into the house with Harper. They were both filthy from the garden, Harper because she had been turning over the earth and had joyfully found scoopful after scoopful of worms, which she brought over to share with Penpen, who had begun to work again in the garden when it became unbearable not to. Harper was developing worm plans.

"Oh my God, look at this one!" Harper cried, holding up one that squirmed and wiggled in her fingers. And they would shriek in delight. The worms were like a miracle, Harper thought, like a whole army of undergardeners spending the night tirelessly turning over the earth for her, aerating it. It felt and smelled that morning like dough when the yeast has been activated, fertile, light, preparing for life. She would not know for years, until Dr Fielding told her so, that this was how pregnant women smelled, too.

When Penpen and Harper came in she could smell it on herself and Penpen still, a kind of gardener's perfume, a kind of baptism by earth. They were smeared with it. Harper thought she could feel it in her nostrils. As though she were still connected to it, an imperishable happiness. Penpen felt strengthened by it, too, nourished by Harper's great energy in the garden. They came in bubbling over and almost didn't notice the threesome sitting glumly around the dining room table.

"Ratchet's in the kitchen making tea," said Tilly, whose fingers itched for the sherry decanter.

Penpen took in Tilly's unusual tea attire, the worn and drawn faces of the man and woman clearly straining to make conversation, and she blurted out, "Oh my goodness, we'd forgotten all about you."

Seniler and seniler, thought Henriette. "Penpen, dear," she said, getting up and extending a hand. Hutch got up, too, but kept his hand to himself as if wary of the appearance of more flailing towels.

"Right!" said Hutch. "Right. Goo doome you."

For a second Penpen thought he was speaking a foreign language. Henriette, who'd had a trying day on planes and then driving the rental car down the long, winding, rutted roads, dodging bears, felt like slapping him. She knew he became more coherent the more relaxed he became, but around this house that might never happen. Anyhow, she thought, disgusted, why should she worry what *they* thought about *him*. They should be worried about what *he* thought of *them*. Especially Ratchet. She should be very worried. Henriette hoped it would keep her on her toes.

When Ratchet brought in the tea, someone finally remembered to introduce Harper. Tilly did it brusquely because she considered Harper none of their business. It was bad enough, she thought, that someone had allowed Henriette to get her hands on one child. She wasn't handing over a second for Henriette's scrutiny. She almost told Harper to take her tea and run for her life, but Harper was eyeing Hutch and Henriette with a certain wary fascination, as you would dangerous reptiles. Henriette was telling stories. Endless stories of the Hunt Club with lots of asides about people whom none of them knew and who seemed to have nothing to do with the stories. Penpen had a smile glued to her face and was attempting as best she could to look interested. Tilly narrowed her eyes and fought to keep from going to the liquor cabinet or falling asleep on the table. When she did neither, it was noted by all except Hutch, who looked restless, as if he were thinking of other things, and Henriette, who was babbling on, unconscious of them all.

Ratchet passed Hutch the cookies, and when for the third time he handed them on without taking one, Tilly interrupted Henriette's story by standing up and declaring, "They're very good cookies!"

They were the last of the cookies that Penpen had made and frozen before her heart attack. Although she cooked meals, she had

169

stopped baking, and the thought that Penpen might be too sick to ever bake again had given Tilly a lot of pain. So much pain that she had begun to revere these last cookies and was mortally offended that anyone would pass them up. It was like being passed the wine at the Last Supper and saying, No thanks, I'm a teetotaller.

"Hutch doesn't eat cookies, Aunt Tilly," said Henriette. "He only eats whole grains, fruits, and vegetables."

"That's a ridiculous way to eat!" said Tilly.

"I'm in training," said Hutch, whose sentences were becoming more audible.

"You're what?" snapped Tilly, who was still mad about the cookies.

"He's in training," said Henriette. "Hutch is the men's World Aerobic Dance Champion."

"The *what*?" said Tilly. Honestly, for years and years there was nothing but the woods and the ocean and an occasional bit of news in town, and then your house was filled with people who brought you word of all kinds of things. More than you could process, more than you could digest. How do people keep up with it all, she thought. How do they have lives with all this clutter in the way?

"It's a kind of sport," said Henriette. "You have to be very talented. You have to train very hard, don't you, Hutch?"

Hutch nodded enthusiastically and drank a sip of his tea. He didn't drink tea, but he didn't want them to think he was *too* much of a pain in the neck. He really just wanted a glass of water but was afraid the tea had some mysterious importance to Tilly, too.

"It requires dance ability, strength, flexibility. Once you're in the national finals, you have to have professional coaching, but I make up all my own routines! I'd been working on making it to the national finals for the last five years, and then two months before I went in, Mother died."

"Oh no!" said everyone but Henriette, who looked annoyed. She liked to be the one to explain things, and the subject of Hutch's mother was an irritant.

"Yes, but I kept training and I won. I dedicated my win to her. She would have been so proud."

Hutch was so excited about his sport that he lost the last of the marble mouth. Now that they could understand him, he didn't seem so menacingly peculiar.

"What do you do exactly? I still don't understand," said Tilly, sounding less annoyed.

"Well, here, I'll show you. I don't suppose you have any music?" Penpen shook her head.

"Well, don't sweat it, darling," said Hutch and went into the centre of the living room, where he began leaping about, falling to impossible postures, and springing up again.

Tilly watched with fascination. She had never seen anything like it. It certainly wasn't dance as she knew it. It wasn't anything as she knew it. It was neither graceful nor charming, and yet Hutch was clearly very pleased with himself in a modest way. When he sat down, Penpen said, "My!"

"I've never met a world champion anything," said Tilly, who actually thought it a silly freakish sport if sport it was, but who felt compelled to acknowledge him in some way.

"Well, we all have our talents," said Hutch modestly. "I bet you're a world champion gardener."

"Actually, Penpen is the gardener," said Tilly.

"Never you mind, dear," said Hutch expansively. "We all, *all* of us have our inner talents and abilities. My mother always said Be the Best You Can Be."

"Can I get your autograph?" asked Harper, who had always wanted to meet someone whose autograph might be valuable.

Hutch beamed, then said suddenly, "I can do better than that. Come with me, both of you." He gestured to Harper and Ratchet and strutted out of the room with them at his heels. When they came back the girls showed Penpen and Tilly what they had. Hutch had given them both a poster with a picture of himself in his leotard receiving his World Aerobic Dance Champion trophy. Across it he had scrawled for each girl, *Be the Best You Can Be.* Tilly and Penpen made the appropriate noises. Hutch was almost overcome and blinked several times. "That's what my mother said to me before she died," he said. "She always believed in me."

Henriette put her cup down sharply and said, "Hutch and I are thinking of becoming engaged." Hutch's mouth fell open.

Harper, who had gone back to eating cookies with a distracted expression ever since she had received her signed poster, had been thinking that perhaps she wasn't being the best she could be, being a good gardener. She felt something else calling her. "It's worms," she thought aloud.

Everyone turned and looked at her. Henriette was furious at being eclipsed, but they couldn't help it. They liked Harper better.

"Yes, dear?" said Penpen patiently. "It is?"

"Good gardens are full of them." She was still excited by the handfuls and handfuls they had found that afternoon. It had sparked something in her, and now Hutch's dead mother, all the way down in Florida, had found her way up on a poster, via Hutch, to further kindle the spark.

"Our garden is certainly full of them," said Penpen.

"But what do we actually know about them?" asked Harper. "Do people give any thought to them other than that they're there?"

"What do you mean?"

"Something that's so vital to a garden's health – what do we really know about them? Are the worms in our garden the best they can be? Suppose there is an optimum kind of worm for a certain kind of garden, for what you're growing, for the kind of soil you have."

Penpen nodded. It did not escape her notice that Harper said "our garden" and she worried vaguely again about Tilly's declining health and her own.

"Shouldn't someone be studying this? Shouldn't someone DO something with this?"

"I really don't know," said Penpen. "How about you?"

"Exactly," said Harper, nodding enthusiastically, happy that Penpen had picked up on her train of thought. "How about me? I have found my life's work. This is a big moment. Pass me the cookies." She shoved one into her mouth as if the idea had made her ravenous, and then she turned to Tilly and said, "If you

173

had a computer I could start researching right now. I really wish you were plugged in." She shoved a second cookie into her mouth.

Henriette was sitting back in her chair looking angry because no one had said anything about their prospective engagement. Ratchet looked frightened. Hutch looked mildly stunned. Tilly was ignoring Henriette's announcement and Harper was thinking about her worms. Only Penpen had the grace to turn to Henriette at last and say, "I'm so sorry. What was this you were saying about getting engaged?"

"I said we were thinking of it," answered Henriette coldly.

"To each other?" asked Penpen in surprise.

Henriette just looked at her. She was on the verge of being unpleasant. Normally she would have been very unpleasant by now, but Ratchet noticed that she seemed to be reining herself in around Hutch.

"Hmmm," said Tilly and stood up to clear the table.

"Don't do that, Aunt Tilly," said Henriette. She had stopped calling everyone dear. It was not an affectation she could keep up. "Ratchet will clear. Ratchet!"

Ratchet jumped up to take away the cups. Harper would have offered to help, but she was thinking of some worm questions to look up the next time she was around Dr Richardson's computer, and so she wandered off in search of pen and paper.

Henriette stood up and said, "Well, I think Hutch and I will go for a swim now. Ratchet! Hurry up. You can come with us and watch!"

Hutch and Henriette went upstairs to change. As Ratchet passed through the living room, Tilly hissed, "Watch nothing! You get in!"

Harper, bent over the "W" volume of the encyclopedia, didn't look up but gave the thumbs-up sign, and Penpen looked worried.

Hutch and Henriette came down and Henriette tapped her toes on the porch until she saw Ratchet. "What are you doing with a towel?" she snapped at Ratchet. "You know you can't swim."

"I thought I would just wade," stuttered Ratchet.

"I'll teach her to swim," said Hutch.

"You'll do nothing of the sort," snapped Henriette. "You're here for a vacation. Ratchet doesn't want to learn to swim. Besides, who can learn in one lesson?" They trudged down the hill.

Well, thank God, thought Tilly, watching them disappear over the crest, now I can have a drink.

At the bottom of the cliff, Hutch and Henriette flung off their clothes and raced into the water, lifting their knees high and running like colts let out of the barn. Ratchet slowly removed her sweater and T-shirt. Underneath was a piece of gauze over the sutures where That Thing had been. She knew it would hurt to have salt water splash on it. The wound was less than a week old. But she decided she didn't care, she was so excited to show Henriette, if she could only get her to pay attention. She stood in her swimsuit watching Henriette and Hutch diving through the waves. She slowly started to walk toward the water when Henriette, her head bobbing up from a dive, spotted her and made a loud gasping noise and came springing on to the beach.

"WHAT ARE YOU DOING?" she hissed, grabbing a towel and flinging it over Ratchet's shoulders. "What in God's name are you doing?" And then she spied the gauze and her mouth made an O.

Ratchet reached back and pulled away the gauze. "I had it removed," she said.

After the tea things were all cleared, Tilly and Penpen moved to the front porch. Harper sat on the porch steps, shelling peas for dinner. The sun was a lovely diffused peach-coloured orb, a misted roundness with no clear definition, sitting softly just over and behind the tops of the pines. The air smelled of leftover woodsmoke from the fires they lit in the woodstove at night, pine needles baking in the sun, and, in gusts, the smell of the sea. They were quiet for a long time. Tilly had moved the sherry out to a table next to her and was pouring herself little glasses but had a cushion handy behind which to hide the bottle should Hutch and Henriette appear on the horizon. Finally Ratchet and Henriette and Hutch appeared. They went upstairs to change. Hutch and Henriette stayed upstairs to take a nap, but Ratchet came down and sat next to Harper, helping her shell.

Penpen was rocking gently back and forth. "Why," she said finally, wonderingly, "did none of us respond very much when she said they were getting engaged?"

Ratchet didn't say anything.

"I know just what you mean," said Tilly, "because without thinking I almost said, 'Oh no you're not,' but I have no idea why that popped into my head. After all, I hardly know Henriette any more."

"Exactly," said Penpen. "And yet I was quite sure they wouldn't get engaged. I'm surprised they're even together. If they are. I don't know why I doubt even that. It's very odd. What do you think, Ratchet?"

."I don't know," said Ratchet. "They seem to like each other. They came all the way here together."

"But you know what we mean, don't you, Ratchet, dear," said Penpen. "It isn't just spite on my part, I hope. For some reason I can't make any of it seem real and I can't put my finger on it."

"Oh for *heaven's* sake," said Harper in exasperation. "Don't you know why?"

And suddenly they did.

THE CANNING SEASON

Two things happened that week that changed the atmosphere in the house. One was having Hutch around. They weren't used to having a man about and it was a great luxury just to have the muscle power. He could and willingly did push Penpen up and down from the sea in the wheelbarrow, so that, for the first time since Penpen's heart attack, Tilly and Penpen were able to indulge in their dips in the sea together, taking turns standing in the waves, holding on to Hutch, who was like a giant bald-headed breakwater. He even drove into town and brought them their mail, which included their order of canning jars.

"I hadn't planned on using them this year," said Penpen. "I was going to leave them at the post office."

Harper wanted to try canning some of the baby vegetables in the garden. They discussed it at dinner one night and Penpen was happy to allow it.

"After all," she said, "it's not as if we'll be using the jars for berries this year."

"Why not?" asked Ratchet, who was feeling a little more relaxed because Hutch had taken her mother out to dinner in Dairy.

"We can't possibly, not this year," said Penpen. "Last year it was hard enough."

"But Harper and I can," said Ratchet.

"Wait a second before we go offering Harper around," said Harper irritably, spearing some carrots on a fork. She had picked them just before dinner and barely steamed them and they still tasted of the earth. "Harper is putting in pretty long days in the garden as it is."

"Besides," said Penpen, "one of you would have to pick."

"And one would have to handle the shotgun," said Tilly. "And it's no good unless one of you can shoot."

Harper stopped eating. "I could learn to shoot," she said.

"Holding the shotgun is the worst job. It's hot . . . it's boring. . ."

"You just stand there. . ." said Penpen.

"Not me, I'd shoot at bees," said Harper.

"Even so," said Tilly.

"Ratchet's right," said Harper, doing an about-face suddenly. "And if we made enough money on the canning sales we could buy a computer and I could start researching worms."

"A computer!" said Tilly scathingly. "Over my dead body."

Then, mid-week, they had to make up their minds because Penpen, coming in from the bogs where she still routinely made checks out of force of habit or perhaps wishful thinking that her picking career wasn't quite over, walked excitedly through the door of the kitchen and announced, "THEY'RE RIPE!" and they had to make a sudden decision. The canning season was on.

From then on in, Ratchet and Harper and Penpen, who was supervising and teaching them, had no time to notice Henriette and Hutch, who came up dutifully for meals to find food had been madly flung on the table and Penpen and Harper and Ratchet were either in the bogs or in the kitchen, splashed with blue juice and sugar and answering in monosyllables, if at all. Tilly was lying on the couch, where she spent all her days now, and would have been hospitable except she didn't want to be and would close her eyes whenever they walked in the room, even though she, like the others, liked Hutch and didn't want to lump him in with Henriette, but it was impossible not to since they were always together. Henriette kept Hutch on a tight leash.

After three days of canning frenzy, Henriette announced coldly that they would have to be leaving. Penpen had invited Henriette to take part in the canning, but Henriette eschewed the whole "messy, sugary, frenetic business". Ratchet thought that the frenetic energy of the canning season was the part she loved best. From dawn to dusk they were swept up in it, connected by the lightning-fast action of the picking and the processing, filling the jars, stirring the great mixture, racing into town for yet more sugar, movement ceasing only for sleep. It was like being a wave in a great ocean. But when Henriette announced abruptly that they were leaving, Ratchet looked crushed and left the jam pot long enough to say goodbye on the porch.

"We're driving down the coast a bit before flying back," said Hutch.

"I think you all work too hard," said Henriette, "scurrying here and there. . ." She had only begun to voice her opinion when Ratchet, who had one ear cocked for the sound of jam boiling over, heard it fizzing in an ominous way and realized it would burn if she didn't move fast. "Oh, wait, I'll be right back. . ." she said, but by the time she returned, they were gone.

The days had gotten so warm that they ate their picnic-style meals out on the porch in the evening, taking their only break in the day to wiggle their toes and cool off from the heat of the kitchen and the bogs. It was a couple of days after Hutch and Henriette had left that Harper turned to Ratchet and said, "Hey, you never told us what happened when your mother saw that thing was gone."

"She said she thought the doctor had botched the job and it was going to leave a nasty scar," said Ratchet. "And that I shouldn't let Hutch see it."

"As if anyone could have done a better job than Dr Richardson!" said Penpen.

"Jeez," said Harper. "Your mother—"

"Harper and Ratchet," interrupted Penpen, "would you mind terribly going into the kitchen and getting Tilly a little more cheese? And something for me."

"What do you want?" asked Harper.

"I really don't care, dear," said Penpen. "As long as it doesn't have blueberries in it."

"Well, amen to that," said Harper as the girls went inside.

They had been working at a furious pace, and Penpen was just leaning back to close her eyes to the evening breeze for a few moments when Tilly uttered a weak cry. Penpen started in alarm. Tilly was slumping in her chair. Penpen arose and leaned over her, unable to utter a sound.

"Listen, Penpen," said Tilly urgently, looking up at her, "I know what we always said we would do, but you know we can't do that now, don't you?"

Penpen nodded vigorously. Now that it was happening, she couldn't believe it. She couldn't believe it and yet it was as if time had stopped and this moment was filling space for miles around. "And, Penpen," said Tilly, her weak voice wild with fear that she wouldn't be able to say it in time, "Penpen, get the phone line changed." Penpen nodded vigorously again and then just stared in agony at Tilly. For years afterward she would wake in the middle of the night, mortified by not having said anything, by being too shocked and frightened and overcome to say any of the things you want to say at such a moment. And then the moment that had lasted so long, had filled so much space, was over.

When Ratchet and Harper came back, Penpen was sitting very quietly. The girls looked at her and then at Tilly and then sat down and for a long time no one said anything at all.

Dr and Mrs Richardson were there and Myrtle Trout and Burl, Penpen, of course, and Ratchet and Harper. They put Tilly next to her mother beneath the gravestone her father had picked out for her seventy-three years before. The morning of the burial, as they waited for the others to arrive, Penpen told Ratchet a story. They had stopped canning for a day and Harper was out weeding the garden.

"You know, I remember burying Mother. It was also during the canning season. This was before we were doing blueberries, but our cook still canned the vegetables from our much bigger kitchen garden and I would help. I always loved gardening and canning. I was just like Harper, the feel of the soil in my hands helped carry me past many things. It was much harder for Tilly. Mother was the thing that carried her past things, and when Mother killed herself Tilly just couldn't understand how she could have left her that way. She didn't see how Mother wouldn't have known or cared that she was the thing that got her through. Tilly couldn't understand any of it. She just wouldn't see Mother as anything but Mother. She was so angry with her. She didn't want Mother to be that way. But the truth was that that summer Mother couldn't be anyone's mother. And, I often think, the truth isn't good or bad, it's just the truth. Tilly wanted Mother in a role that Mother hadn't been able to sustain, I guess. I wasn't angry at Mother. Of course, I was sad. We were both so sad. And it was horrible to trip on her head."

"You actually tripped over it?" said Ratchet.

"Right over it. Got blood on the toe of this shoe," said Penpen, holding up her right foot as if she could still see it there. "Tilly seemed to think that she must have burdened Mother in some way, so she would stay here in the woods and never burden anyone else.

People can be hurt so badly that they choose to just stop in their tracks. I think that's why she chose those Emily Dickinson verses for her wedding. Before Burl even started blathering on with those silly vows of his, she was warning him, don't disturb this ground. I'm happy to be burying her there next to Mother. I think she thought that next to Mother was where she would find her peace, so I hope she was right, but I fear, Ratchet, that where we find our peace is in ourselves. And I think part of her feared that if Mother could leave her that way, she must be unlovable. And of course, she wasn't." Penpen's face screwed up for a moment. "I loved her." Penpen didn't cry, but Ratchet, looking at her wistful face, wished she would.

At the graveside, Penpen said that Tilly lived the way she had chosen, in the woods, uncluttered and undisturbed, and that we have to love people as they are, free from what we want them to be. Then she recited the verses Tilly had once chosen for herself:

> Ample make this bed.
> Make this bed with awe;
> In it wait till judgment break
> Excellent and fair.
>
> Be its mattress straight,
> Be its pillow round;
> Let no sunrise' yellow noise
> Interrupt this ground.

They all stood quietly. Myrtle, looking at Tilly's grave, said, "I would have put her in a few inches more to the right."

Then they went back to the canning.

Penpen had the phone line fixed so that they could phone out, and when they guessed Henriette and Hutch had returned to Pensacola, Ratchet phoned her mother. When she told her about Tilly's death, Henriette said, "Well, that's not what you'd call a big surprise."

"And Penpen got the phone fixed so we can call out now," said Ratchet.

"It's about time for that, too," sniffed Henriette. She seemed unusually sniffy, so Ratchet asked her if anything was wrong and she said, "Well, you may as well know, I'm not seeing Hutch any more."

"Oh," said Ratchet. "I'm sorry."

"He was becoming intolerable. All that leaping about all the time. All that exercise. All that brown rice."

"So I guess that's why I was able to reach you at home," said Ratchet.

"Anyhow, Ratchet, I'm off to work. I suppose Penpen will want to cut your visit short now."

"She hasn't said anything about it. In fact, Harper is staying on and home-schooling."

"What nonsense," said Henriette. "Penpen can't teach anything. She's senile. Look, I really do have to run."

The next day Ratchet phoned Henriette because she was

worried that her mother was wandering around the house alone and sad.

"Hi, Mom," she said.

"You *again*!" said her mother. "Didn't you just call yesterday?"

Ratchet hung up and went into the kitchen, where Penpen and Harper were boiling sugar and filling jars. "Penpen, do you think I could stay the winter, too?"

Penpen looked at her and said, "Well, of course, dear. Oh dear, someone grab some pot holders. Rescue that pot before it boils over, Harper!" And no one ever brought it up again, although Henriette called several times to tell Ratchet she was making a big mistake. They kept finding her messages telling her so on the answering machine Harper had made them buy, but because they were usually out in the garden or with the bees or picking the last of the berries, no one was around to answer the phone and Ratchet never called her mother back.

"How long do you think you are going to stay?" asked Harper one day out in the field.

"I was hoping no one would ask that question," said Ratchet.

"Me too," said Harper.

They finished the harvest, Penpen planted seeds on Tilly's grave, and after that canning season, she taught Ratchet and Harper to drive.

EPILOGUE

Penpen stayed alive until the girls turned eighteen and nineteen; then that summer, during the canning season, in accordance with family tradition, Penpen died. The girls and Dr Richardson put her in the ground. Dr Richardson, who was beginning to shake with Parkinson's now, stood quivering next to them at graveside.

Penpen had left the house and all her worldly goods to the two girls, who had spent the last few years being home-schooled. Hutch came every summer to visit, and when he heard of Penpen's death, he came up with a whole set of home gym equipment for both of them. He was no longer a tennis pro at the Hunt Club but had followed his first love of aerobic dance and was successfully training other hopeful world champions.

"But I'm no good at relationships," he said sadly.

"When would you have *time* for them?" the girls protested, because they knew he worked his ageing body relentlessly to stay on top of things.

"I do see your mother around town from time to time," said Hutch.

"Oh yes," said Ratchet. Her mother had never been to see her after she chose to stay in the woods.

"I think she was having a romance with someone a bit more, shall we say, suitable, for a while?" said Hutch. "I did have hopes. I really did, but last time I saw her she had dumped him, too. 'You have to stop this, Henriette!' I said to her."

"Well, Mother doesn't like change," said Ratchet.

"And *you're* going off to college!" said Hutch to Harper, who had just been accepted to Bowdoin for the fall. "What are *you* going to do all alone in the woods? You should go, too," said Hutch, turning to Ratchet.

"No, I like the woods," said Ratchet. It was all she had known for years, but she worried that maybe the idea of college didn't appeal because she, like her mother, just didn't like change. It bothered her.

"That's what I keep saying," said Harper. "Suddenly instead of three of us together, you'll be alone. It's not going to be the same. You're going to get strange."

This became the recurring refrain after Harper moved to Brunswick and began her college year. She would come home whenever she could spare a weekend away and at some point would always begin, "You are going to get strange."

"Well, do I seem strange yet?" she asked Harper.

"The year is young," said Harper darkly. "Nobody will ever find you in the woods. Don't you want to have babies and children? Don't you want to *do it* with a man?"

188

"I love our farm," said Ratchet soundly. They now sold products besides their canned blueberries. She was experimenting with cheese and selling honey and honey products. "Besides, if someone is meant to find me, they can find me in the woods as well as anywhere else."

"Fairy tales!" scoffed Harper. "Nobody is going to find you in the woods. You have to go out there where the guys *are*. Hey, wouldn't you just like to go to Bowdoin with me for a week? See what it's like? Meet some guys?" Harper was forever meeting guys. She seemed made for it. Romances bloomed and died on a weekly basis. When Ratchet shook her head, Harper looked as if she would explode. "You know you *could* go away for a few years. We'll always have the house. We'll never sell it." This was the pact they had made when Penpen died. No matter what happened to either of them, no matter where life took them, they would never sell the house.

"What should I be out there looking for?" asked Ratchet. "I found what I like. I want to keep bees and take care of cows and can the blueberries." But she wondered if Harper was right and that maybe she was staying in the woods for the wrong reasons.

One day she was puttering around the cemetery when the phone rang and she dashed in. It was Hutch, who called periodically to check on her and ask her what she was up to. "I was trying to figure out something to plant on Penpen's grave," said Ratchet. "I just thought it would be pretty in the spring if there were some flowers there or something."

"Why don't you plant what she planted on Tilly's grave?"

189

"What is that awful stuff?" asked Ratchet, chomping on leftover toast as she gazed out the window.

"You're supposed to be the gardener," said Hutch.

"I just figured it was some kind of weed."

"It's mustard. Penpen loved mustard seed. She said you could scatter it anywhere and it often took root even in the most inhospitable ground."

"Oh, that Penpen, she just loved to plant," said Ratchet.

"She just loved to plant," agreed Hutch.

Harper finished college and became a famous worm expert. Also an expert on organic gardening with pests. She doctored gardens all over New England, had six babies, leaving them at home with her novelist husband while she travelled, her hands always dipping into other people's soil, like coming home, like feeling in the heart of the earth, her heart, everyone's heart. They brought the children to visit Ratchet, and Harper would say to her as she'd been saying for fifteen years, "Aren't you worried you'll get strange out here by yourself?"

One day, when Ratchet was beginning to worry about this herself, there was a knock on her door. When she answered it, a man stood there next to a pregnant woman. Ratchet understood immediately that for the second time in Glen Rosa's hundred-year history, someone had kept going after taking the wrong turn-off from Dink. She began patiently explaining where he had gone wrong and giving him the proper directions to the orphanage when she found herself arrested by his toplock of hair, which was blond and curled upward from his forehead in a most enticing manner.

She immediately gave herself a little shake, as this man was already taking one pregnant woman to St Cyr's. This was no time to start anything, she said to herself. Perhaps she *was* getting strange. Later that evening the man returned but without the pregnant woman, who anyway turned out to be his sister, and this time he had not lost his way. His name was Richard Fielding and he stayed for fifty-some years before joining the rest of the crew under the mustard plants. Richard Fielding was a doctor and he loved the woods, so the pregnant, the sick, the loggers of Dink were once again cared for. Mrs Richardson had died without being able to get to Florida, but Dr Richardson could finally sit down and rest, and Dr Fielding took care of him, too.

For many years Harper would return during the canning season, coming to help, and then she and her husband would take a holiday alone, leaving the children with Ratchet and her husband.

During one such stay Ratchet had the baby, Tutu, on her lap. Emily, Ramona, Theresa, Tilly, and Penny, Harper's other daughters, were sitting at the table eating their blueberry muffins from the bunny plates "Aunt Ratchet" had bought them when the phone rang. It was Henriette. Ratchet and Henriette still called each other once or twice a year. She had her usual short conversation with Henriette.

When Ratchet hung up, Emily, who was twelve, said, "Was that Henriette?" Ratchet nodded. "If you were really our aunt, then she would be our great-aunt, right?"

"I am really your aunt," said Ratchet complacently, helping herself to another muffin.

"How come she never visits in the summer when we're here?" Emily had heard stories about Henriette from her mother, but she wanted to hear what Ratchet had to say. Ratchet suspected as much and thought about it for a minute. "Well, Henriette doesn't travel well. She doesn't like change."

"Mom says she doesn't like *you*," said Emily.

Ratchet thought about that for a minute. "You know what Henriette likes? The Hunt Club."

"Like that grace you taught us? *That* Hunt Club?" asked Emily.

"Yes."

"What's the Hunt Club?" asked Ramona.

"It's this wonderful place where you can play tennis and swim in this azure pool and ride horses and all the drinks come with little umbrellas in them."

"Why did she say thank God for that?"

"Because that's the place she always wanted to go, I guess. That's what she thought about when she waited tables and cleaned apartments for other people. She just wanted someday to be a member of the Hunt Club."

"Mom said that Henriette thought you kept her out of the Hunt Club and that made you so mad you didn't talk to her for years," said Emily.

Ratchet's face tightened for a minute, then suddenly she was grateful for Penpen, Tilly, Harper, and Henriette. It was as if they had all made a promise to come into this life bringing with them all their own information, as if where they had been, what they needed, what they knew, all their stories, was fission, creating critical mass, so that, at one point, she would glean a small nugget of understanding. She thought how Penpen's batteries were constantly being recharged not because she was loved but because love moved so fluidly through her. How she allowed herself this like a great gift. "The truth is Henriette just wanted the Hunt Club desperately for both of us. Then I found I had to get away from Henriette and her idea of the Hunt Club, and that made both of us very, very sad and sometimes it's easier for people to be angry than to be sad. But I never stopped worrying that she couldn't get in. One year during the canning season, after, I guess, I had spent just about enough time worrying about it, and while, as your mother would be happy to point out, I was supposed to be filling jars with jam, I called them and they said that anyone could be a member, you, me, Henriette. There is no difficulty. It was never up to me to get anyone in. And then I stopped worrying."

The day was sunny and warm. Ratchet's husband was in the lumber camps doing the foot rounds, checking the loggers' feet for festering blisters and fungi. Ratchet knew he would be gone a long time because the loggers didn't like to take off their boots and reveal their sores and wounds and embarrassing fungi. Richard had to spend a lot of time assuring them that their feet were not shameful, there was no such thing as good feet or bad feet, they were just feet. But because he had to go through this process with nearly every logger, Ratchet knew it would be a long day, so she planned a late lobster dinner for all of them and after lunch took the children down to the ocean.

It was a perfect summer day; the air was soft and sparkling

opaquely blue with sea spray. Everyone stayed in the water swimming for ever, waves crashing over them, whitecaps frosting the water, as they bounced in their various corners of the sea. Emily, who was splashing Ramona with giddy abandon, shouted above the waves, "Thank God for the Hunt Club!"

"Yes, the Hunt Club," cried Ramona.

"Thank God for that," said Tilly, who was floating around blissfully on an inflated dinosaur.

"Yes," said Penny, wading along the shore.

"Where would we be without it?" said Emily.

"Nowhere, that's where," said Ramona.

"Well, thank God for it," said Emily. "Yep, that's for sure."

A wave broke over Ratchet, drenching her, water running into her eyes and mouth and over her naked shoulders. "Yep," she repeated, "that's for sure."

Then they all swam long and hard and afterward went up to the house to have dinner with Dr Fielding, and after dinner Ratchet went out under the peach-coloured sky to tend the bees, floating happily from barn to chicken house to the garden, moving peacefully forward in the soft summer haze.

Have you read

everything
on a
waffle

by Polly Horvath?

I live in Coal Harbour, British Columbia. I have never lived anyplace else. My name is Primrose Squarp. I am eleven years old. I have hair the colour of carrots in an apricot glaze (recipe to follow), skin fair and clear where it isn't freckled, and eyes like summer storms.

One June day a typhoon arose at sea that blew the rain practically perpendicular to our house. My father's fishing boat was late getting in and my mother, who wasn't one for sitting around biting her nails, put on her yellow macintosh and hat and took me over to Miss Perfidy's house, saying, "Miss Perfidy, John is out there somewhere and I don't know if his boat is coming safely into shore, so I am going out in our sailboat to find him." Well, a thinking person might have told my mother that if a big fishing boat wasn't going to make it through those waves, our little skiff sure wasn't. But Miss Perfidy wasn't one to waste time in idle chitchat. She just nodded. And that was the last I saw of my mother.

The fishing boat never came back to shore. Neither did the skiff. So all that June I continued to live with Miss Perfidy. There was a memorial service for my parents but I wouldn't go. I knew that my parents hadn't drowned. I suspected that they had washed up on an island somewhere and were waiting to be rescued. Every morning I went down to the docks to watch the boats come in, sure that I would see my parents towed in, perhaps on the back of a whale.

"I don't know what you think the story of Jonah is

about, Miss Perfidy," I said. "But to me it is about how hopeful the human heart is. I am certain my parents, if not in the belly of a whale, are wondering how I am doing and trying to get home to me!" I called the last few words out in the direction Miss Perfidy had gone. She often stalked off when I was in the middle of a sentence. It didn't encourage many heartfelt confidences.

I didn't mind Miss Perfidy's exits, but what I did mind was her mothball smell, which was never overwhelming yet hovered around her in a little fog. Mothballs spilled from every drawer in her house. I couldn't understand why Miss Perfidy seemed to be the only person in town who had such a huge problem with moths. One day I got out a box and read the directions. "You know, Miss Perfidy," I said, "is it possible that you misunderstood the directions? You seem to be using an awful *lot* of mothballs." But Miss Perfidy had already left the room.

Besides, it wasn't really any of my business. The town council was paying Miss Perfidy her usual baby-sitting fee of three dollars an hour from what they called the Squarps' estate and what I called my parents' bank account until they could figure out what to do with me. This was taking them a lot longer than it might have because my parents hadn't made wills or thought ahead to the day when they would both disappear at sea. But even I knew that at three dollars an hour I wasn't long for life with Miss Perfidy.

One member of the town council argued that three dollars an hour was a lot to pay a baby-sitter for those endless night hours when I was asleep and Miss Perfidy was snoring in her own bed, but it was fruitless to argue with Miss Perfidy. She was mean with money. In Coal Harbour there was whaling and fishing and the navy. If you didn't whale or fish or do naval things you had to do what you could to hold body and soul together, so Miss Perfidy was tight with her pennies by necessity. When things had got too tight a few years back she had sold her small cottage and bought an even smaller cottage. Before she moved from the small cottage she dug up her flower bulbs one by one – tulips, daffodils, crocuses – and not being a real stinker, neatly filled in all the holes again. When the estate agent heard about it, he came charging over. "Miss Perfidy," he had said. "You just can't do this. People expect you to *leave* your flowers." But she said she had paid for and planted every last bulb and she was taking every last bulb, and speaking of bulbs she was also unscrewing and taking all the lightbulbs. Land's sakes, did he want her to leave her clothes for the new owners too?

Melissa Public Library
Melissa, Texas

Melissa Public Library
Melissa, Texas